DEATH OF A MYTH MAKER

DEATH

OF A

MYTH MAKER

Allana Martin

THOMAS DUNNE BOOKS
St. Martin's Minotaur 🐂 New York

The characters and events depicted in this book are fictitious. Any re-semblance to real persons, living or dead, is coincidental. Presidio County, Texas, and Chihuahua State, Mexico, are real political and geographic entities. However, for purposes of plot and storytelling, not all places named are real, nor are real places always as described.

THOMAS DUNNE BOOKS.
An imprint of St. Martin's Press.

ISBN 0-312-25241-2

Map by Mark Stein

First Edition: March 2000

10   9   8   7   6   5   4   3   2   1

In memory of my aunt, Iris Powell

Humans are the only ones among God's creatures that discern good and evil, and the only ones that need to.

—Father Jack Raff

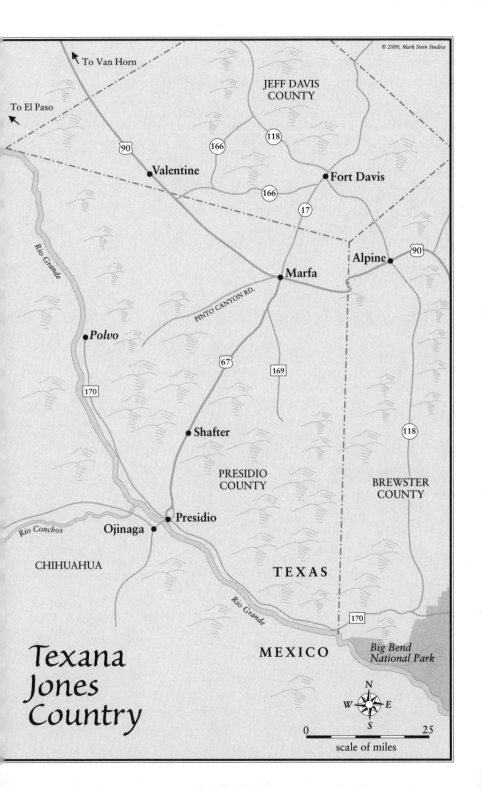

DEATH

OF A

MYTH MAKER

PROLOGUE

An entry, dated only early October, 1852, written by John Asher Hearne, excerpted from *Personal Narrative of a Scalp Hunter,* filed under *Account of the Scalp Hunters of Northern Mexico,* University of Texas Archives, Austin:

> Last night occurred an event that saw us hurriedly break camp and move down the creek from the high grasslands where we had stopped on our way back to La Junta after selling the 200 head of mules, cattle, and horses we had taken along with 55 scalps. I thought never to see the men I am in company with, men who take no quarter and

give none but slice a scalp and plunge their fingers under the skin to rip it from the skull, quake with fear. Even Negrito, the Mescalero who rides with us, and whose purse bulges with newly minted silver coins paid by the governor of the State of Chihuahua for the hundreds of scalps he has hung on the fence in front of the great cathedral in Chihuahua City, knew the strange occurrence boded ill. It happened after sunset as we sat around our campfire, sharpening our knives and roasting chunks of freshly killed game on sticks, Indian fashion. The night was moonless and as black as Flog the Irishman's hair. It was he who first saw them from where he sat hunched over his coffee. He jumped to his feet and shouted, "Indian fires!" Thinking of more scalps for the taking at first light, the men stirred, lifted their heads, and looked to where Flog pointed. Captain Long observed that it looked more like bobbing lanterns to him. Maybe a trader journeying toward La Junta, he reckoned. I tossed out the remainder of my coffee and stood to have a better view. With the Comanche and Apache roaming at will from San Antonio to El Paso, it would take a brave trader to travel the trails hereabouts unless in company of men willing to fight. Whether lanterns or campfires, what I saw appeared to be in the mountains we had traveled toward all day. The objects might have been bright stars, except they appeared too low for stars. When they moved I felt my hair rise like the quills on a porcupine facing down a hound. "Not campfires," said Wahqua, the Spanish boy raised by the Comanche. The shining objects did not move together, but at odds with one another, up and down. Some appeared to float and grow bigger, moving fast and slow, together and apart. By then all the men were on their feet. Flog crossed himself, and Captain Long uttered an oath. Negrito threw down his food and shouted that it was the spirits of his people, lighting fires for the Indians he had scalped to find their way home. He mounted his horse and with a keen yell rode out of camp toward the mountains, brandishing his rifle over his head. By then we were all moving, packing up and getting the horses saddled. Flog led out, not after Negrito, but down the trail following the creek south toward the Rio Grande. Captain Long was the last to leave, kicking dirt over the fire to smother it. I looked aside at the strange sight once again as we rode. Spirits, fires, or lanterns, they danced still. Negrito had vanished into the dark, out of sight and hearing. Nor did we ever see him again.

ONE

I don't see the big deal about this. They look like flashlights to me. I bet it's kids with flashlights."

The man speaking with such certainty leaned his rotund weight against the minivan with New York license plates parked next to my white Ford pickup and waited for his wife to become as bored as he at the display of the Marfa Lights glowing in the darkness against the distant Chinati mountains. Sitting on the tailgate, I could see the lights plainly as they appeared and disappeared.

"It's not flashlights," his equally heavy wife said. "They're glowing real soft in blue and white. Look." She thrust the binoculars at him and dutifully, he looked.

"It's a gimmick for tourists, Blanche. Use your head." He handed back the binoculars. "I'll be in the van."

"Fascinating," my sister-in-law Fran said. "I admit I was skeptical, but this is really something. One is pulling apart as I watch."

Fran stood in the bed of my pickup, her eyes pressed to my binoculars, looking across the Mitchell Flats and toward the mountains. Even with her long, brown hair tied back into a ponytail and dressed in casual clothes, Fran was a striking woman and a stylish one. Everything she wore, from tennis shoes to windbreaker sported a designer label. It was nine-thirty. Along with fourteen other vehicles, we had parked in the Texas Highway Department's viewing area nine miles east of Marfa. The area was filled because it was the Wednesday before the Labor Day weekend and the annual Marfa Lights Festival, which brought a fair share of tourists to stay in the local motels. The Marfa Lights, irregular in their display, were making a showing that kept most of the watchers, even those without binoculars, interested. The five or six lightbulb-size luminaries weren't spectacular, only mysterious and unexplained.

"What's the theory on this?" Fran said.

"The romantic legend is that the lights are signal fires lit by an Apache chief named Alsate to guide his people back to the safety of the mountains."

"They lived there?"

"The Mescalero Apache knew every mountain,

road, arroyo, canyon, and cave around here. They ended up in the Trans-Pecos after being driven out of the Llano Estacado by the Comanche. But everybody, whites, Mexicans, Apache, were afraid of the Comanche. The tribe had made treaty with the United States, but Texas was a republic then and Texans and Mexicans were considered fair game. For over a hundred years, the warriors crossed the Pecos River and swept through west Texas, riding for the Rio Grande and Mexico, raiding for livestock and captives. Not a rancho or village was safe. So many Mexicans were killed or captured that the governor of Chihuahua paid mercenaries to stop the raids. The scalp-hunting bounty was known as Mexico's Fifth Law. Don't ask me what the first four were, I have no idea. Chihuahua paid from one to five hundred pesos for every Indian scalp brought in. We're talking the first half of the nineteenth century when the peso was nearly equivalent to the dollar. A hundred dollars was real wealth in those days. Men, and even a few women, poured in from as far away as Tennessee and Canada. The silver mines at Chihuahua City turned out newly minted silver pesos just to make the scalp payments. Raiding an Indian camp at dawn was like finding a gold mine. So much so, the mercenaries got carried away and took any scalp, friendly Indian, poor Mexican, or fellow mercenary, as long as the hair was black."

Fran lowered the binoculars and gazed at me. "Did it work, the bounty?"

"It slowed the raids, but ended up causing more

trouble. Most of the mercenaries were white, so the Indians turned against all whites, even those they'd made private treaty with. No one was safe, especially when the Civil War took the soldiers out of Fort Davis."

Fran put the binoculars back to her eyes. "Is there any scientific theory about the lights?"

"Natural phenomena of unknown origin," I said. "That's the usual write-up's explanation, which explains nothing. Some people have suggested that it's reflected lights from cars on Highway Sixty-seven, which doesn't explain why the Indians and early settlers saw the lights. Then there are the wilder explanations of iridescent jackrabbits or swamp gas—"

"Swamp gas in a desert?"

"Like I said, theorists."

We watched for nearly thirty minutes, during which time the minivan couple left and a busload of high school kids arrived, grew bored quickly, and left.

Soon after, Fran and I called it quits, as did most of the other watchers. Every vehicle except mine headed east into Alpine, where most of the motels are. Driving west toward Marfa, we had the two-lane highway to ourselves in an empty world. The Trans-Pecos of far west Texas, with its rimrock mesas, arched brown mountains, volcanic calderas, sun-bleached lowlands, and the Rio Grande running through the open valleys and rock canyons, is one of the rare places left where people are insignificant.

My name is Texana Jones, and I live in Presidio

County, Texas, one of the nine counties that make up the Trans-Pecos region. We have maximum land space, 3,855 square miles, and minimum population, just over seven thousand. The county is shaped roughly like a right triangle. The county seat of Marfa is tucked into the northeastern corner. Sixty miles to the southwest, the Rio Grande forms the longest side of the triangle. Right on the river is Presidio. Go up river toward distant El Paso and my trading post is at mile fifty. Polvo, population 125 and one of the county's oldest communities, is at mile fifty-two. After Polvo, the road goes five more miles, but it's only graded lava rock, and washes out after any rainfall, though we get under ten inches a year.

I kept my eyes on the road, looking out for mule deer, pronghorn antelope, javelina on the move under the cover of darkness, as well as the more mundane among our wildlife population such as coyotes, skunks, raccoons, gray foxes, and desert cottontails. Fran made no attempt at conversation, but sat slumped in the seat, her long legs folded up against the dash, her eyes staring at the darkness of the roadside. Such physical lassitude was no part of her normally frenetic personality.

Fran is my husband's only sibling, ten years younger than he, and physically very similar, nearly matching his six-foot, one-inch height and very like him in feature, with hooded gray-green eyes, prominent nose, and strong chin. Fran's hair is the same thick gloss, though hers shows no gray. However much they look alike, in personality the two are opposites. Clay is calm and steady, Fran is nervy and impulsive. A transplant from Fort Worth, Clay had come to Presidio County to get away from people. Fran had majored in interior design, marrying right out of college a promising young attorney named Jake Dare. They soon bought a home in the affluent suburbs of sprawling Houston. Fran produced two children and did the society-charity routine while her husband made a name for himself statewide as a defense attorney, taking on big and bigger cases. Jake Dare. The name evoked the privateering spirit that befitted the most successful of the lawyer breed, and Jake capitalized on it, "Daring to take on the toughest cases Texans can offer," he'd been quoted as saying. In 1998, Jake had been named "one of the twenty most impressive, intriguing, and influential people in Texas" by *Texas Monthly*. Fran sent us a copy of the glossy magazine.

Fran adored her brother Clay, and I thought she was fond of me in a mild way, knowing that Clay was happy in his marriage, but she had never hidden her feelings about our lifestyle. In Fran's eyes, Clay and I, the veterinarian and the trading post owner, were hermits, and without the requisite wealth to qualify as eccentrics, merely odd. In all the years of our marriage, she had paid us only three one-day visits, supplemented by long, chatty telephone calls and punctuated by lavish gifts selected from the trendier catalogs. Fran's asking if she might come and stay for a week had been startling, but from her arrival that afternoon until this moment, she had remained mute on anything but pleasantries.

We had made the last rise on Highway 90. Ahead, the lights of Marfa, the town, glowed softly. Not brightly. The population of the Presidio County seat is just short of three thousand, and because of the McDonald Observatory in the Davis Mountains in the next county over, the entire region avoids overlighting, using guards to deflect outdoor lights downward in order to protect the darkness of the night sky. Marfa showed as a small stretch of lights in the middle of a vast and velvet darkness.

Fran blurted out, "I've left Jake."

Before I could take in her flat statement, Marfa vanished. One second there were lights, the next there was nothing save the ancient light of the stars to distinguish sky from earth. This, I thought, is what it must have looked like before the dawn of the first light. I stopped the truck, rolled down my window, and poked my head out into the cool night air, as if the view would be different from that visible through the windshield. Instead, I heard something that increased my feeling that this was an *X-Files* moment. From out of the darkness flowed a vintage forties dance band accompanied by a mellow voice crooning, "Isn't it romantic." Had I been transported back in time to a World War II blackout? On the road something moved into the edge of the pickup headlights, a dancing couple, the woman's full skirt swirling as her partner finished the turn in a dip.

Fran gave a choked giggle. "Do you see what I see?"

"Do you mean Marfa disappearing or Fred and Ginger waltzing the yellow line?"

"Good, you see them. For a minute I thought my Prozac was making me hallucinate."

The couple stopped and, arm-in-arm, walked toward us.

"I saw them get off a plane at the airport while I was waiting. So you know them?" Fran asked, her voice edgy.

"The woman is Ella Spivey. She belongs to one of the oldest ranching families in the Trans-Pecos. I've never seen her dance partner before." I cut the emergency flashers on, got out, and walked to meet the pair. Behind me, I heard the wail of the Union Pacific train's horn as it rolled west after its stop in Alpine.

"Hello, Texana Jones," Ella's soprano voice called to me over the sound of the music.

Ella wore a paper flower pinned in her upswept white hair, a frilly red blouse with a flared denim skirt, and shiny red boots on her feet. Everything her partner wore, from the black felt western hat to the fancy boots on his small feet, looked new. He looked like a friendly elf playing cowboy.

"We've been dining at Reata in Alpine," Ella said.

"We must have just missed you. I picked up my sister-in-law at the airport and took her to an early dinner, then we drove out to see the Marfa Lights."

"I took Julian to see them when he first arrived in Marfa." Ella introduced her companion as Julian

Row, who smiled, and said, "I've seen similar phenomena in many places all across the globe. Pakistan, India, all the hot, dry climates seem to have mystery lights."

"Julian has led such an exciting life," Ella said.

I said, "The most exciting thing that happens around here are the low-level flights of the German air force training in New Mexico."

"This is a beautiful setting, though," Julian said, looking at Ella and placing his hand over hers where it rested on his arm. "Perfect for a beautiful lady."

He smiled at me like a politician ten points down in the polls. "You caught us out, Texana. We had a flat, and after I changed the tire, I couldn't resist asking Ella to dance with me under the stars."

"Night dancing on Highway Ninety might seem a bit odd to some folks, Julian, but I'll bet Ella has told you about the ranch families that used to meet at the crossroads for dances by headlights. I guess you've got a tape player somewhere in the car, not the whole band."

Julian smiled. "It's on the hood, along with a chilled bottle of champagne. If you'd care for a glass, follow me." He pulled free of Ella's arm to gesture broadly behind him. "Hey! Where has Marfa gone to?"

"Looks like the mayor forgot to pay the light bill," I said. "If you two are okay, I'll be on my way."

"We've never been better," Ella said.

I wished them good night, returned to the pickup,

and drove off, leaving the dancers alone under the stars.

"What are they doing out here?" Fran said as I climbed back into the driver's seat. "Are they crazy or drunk?"

"Neither as far as I can tell, although they have champagne with them," I said, pulling my seat belt tight. "Ella Spivey is one of the seven sisters. You know, like the Pleiades. That would make their daddy Atlas, and from the way they talk about dear departed dad, I'd say they thought he held up the whole world like a god, although judging by the lovey looks Ella was giving her dance partner, it looks like she may have found someone she thinks as much of."

"Explain the Plee-uh-deez."

"It's the name of the constellation. Supposed to be seven sisters, the daughters of the god, Atlas. I guess in Houston you can't see the stars to know them. Anyway, that's the way everyone around here refers to the Spivey sisters and their ranch. It's a beautiful place in high country. Good grass, adequate water, spectacular views. The sisters all live together in one big house that their daddy built. They refer to themselves as 'unmarried ladies,' never 'spinsters' or 'single.' They expect locals to call them by their first names, and outsiders to say, *Miss* Spivey, never Miz. Not one is under sixty. Ella is in the middle, somewhere between Leila and the twins, Hattie and Mattie."

"What about the dance partner," Fran said.

"All I know is his name, Julian Row."

"He's a little over age for a 'toy boy,' " Fran said. She gave me a look. "That's not why I left Jake by the way. I mean, I'm not having an affair."

"I didn't assume you were."

What had happened to her marriage? I thought about Jake's photo in *Texas Monthly*, the hard brown eyes, the raised chin, and the confident smile as he posed surrounded by the media that increasingly covered him rather than his high profile clients. Posture or reality? Was he as arrogant as he looked? I hardly knew the man.

"Are you listening?" Fran was saying.

"I'm sorry, Fran. About you and Jake. Let's get home and we'll talk about it, if that's what you want."

"There's nothing to say, really. I woke up one day, that's all. You might say I was a lot like Miss Spivey back there, dancing with a man on a highway to nowhere."

She paused for breath, and I smiled to myself over her characterization of this being a road to nowhere. The citizenry, most of them anyway, would say that was what made the town a good place to live.

"I'm sick and tired of my whole life," Fran said. "Jake's life, really. On the rare occasion that Jake is home before ten in the evening, we have nothing to say to one another. When we make love, it isn't. It's coupling. The parties we attend are networking events. I want a divorce. The kids are old enough to handle it. Jake said I should think about it, that he is perfectly satisfied with things the way they are. He should be.

Everything and everyone in his world revolves around him. Sounds a lot like Daddy Spivey, the way you described him."

I wanted to throw out a cautionary note about tossing away what you have without due thought, but I didn't say so. People in Fran's situation want support, not advice.

"Let's forget Jake and go find out what has happened to Marfa," Fran said.

TWO

Marfa sits on a high sweep of grassland nearly as high as Denver, landlocked by huge ranches, isolated by inhospitable land forms and limited water. There are no fast-food franchises, only a couple of local restaurants with a chronic need for additional help. The businesses are utilitarian: groceries, gas, insurance, furniture, liquor. Once a waterstop on the Texas and New Orleans railroad, the town hasn't changed much in appearance since it was named after a character in Dostoyevsky's *The Brothers Karamazov* because the railroad engineer's wife happened to be reading the book and liked the name. It is headquarters for a sector of the Border Patrol, home to two art foundations, and a handful of galleries and a number of artists.

We rolled through a town blacked-out except for a few headlights. I stopped on a corner of Highland Street by the Paisano Hotel and asked the shadowy figure of a man on the sidewalk what had happened. "Don't know yet," said a voice I could not place.

I waved a hand in thanks and drove south toward Presidio. Marfa is above the rimrock, Presidio is below. Marfa is Anglo culture, with Rotary, Masons, and Protestant churches. Presidio is Hispanic, with *brujas* and *curanderos* and Catholicism.

"I forget," Fran said, "how far is it to the trading post? I thought we'd gone out of state getting to the spot to see the lights."

"Just over a hundred miles," I said, "but we'll make good time the first fifty."

"How do you stand having to drive fifty or a hundred miles any time you want to go anywhere?"

"You get used to it. Of course, it makes eating out expensive, if you include the cost of the gas. I guess it's a good thing I like to stay home."

"What do you do all day?"

"Nothing much. That's what I enjoy, the quiet, the view of the mountains across the river, bird watching, sitting on the porch and reading. The trading post gets its fair share of customers from the ranches above Pinto Canyon and from the other side of the river. People drop in to visit, buy supplies, pass along the latest news or hear it. It's nice."

"It's so provincial," Fran said.

"Does the *Houston Chronicle* cover your charity events?"

"What do you mean?"

"What do they write about when they cover, say, Houston's big social events like, what do you call it, the Black and Gold Ball?"

"That's the Silver and Gold Ball. The story always has attendees' names, important ones, what the wives wore, how much money was collected for charity, who decorated, and what the decorations were. That sort of thing."

"In other words, things that interest the locals, and only a handful of those. Friendly gossip. Isn't that provincial, too?"

Fran shook her head and looked at me. "You have a contrary mind-set."

"Quirky, my first husband called it."

"I'd forgotten you'd been divorced once. I don't think I've ever heard you talk about it. I don't even know his name. Did you hate him?"

I laughed. "Didn't then, don't now. We were married less than a year. His name was Jeffrey Sanford-Gordy."

Fran sat up out of her slump to stare at me in the glow of the dash lights. "*He* was your first husband? Texana, the man's a multimillionaire. I've read about him in the newspapers, and a couple of magazines, and the *Wall Street Journal*. He's got homes all over the world. Well, the important places, anyway."

"That doesn't surprise me. One of the first things he

told me was that he planned to be a millionaire before he was thirty. I'm glad he made it."

"Oh, he made it. Do you mind if I ask why you divorced him?"

"Mutual relief. Or should that be release? We met our freshman year at the University of Texas. I grew up in Polvo, and today's population of one hundred and twenty-five is bigger than in my childhood. He was a city kid from Dallas. We mistook a healthy sexual attraction for love. At first, we found our differences intriguing. Realistically, I guess each of us thought the other would change. I couldn't become the society wife he wanted, and he wasn't going to live in the desert with me and run a trading post that in a good year breaks even. Living on the edge of an adverb, Clay calls it."

"Meaning what?" Fran asked.

"*About* to go under."

"Your divorce, how did you decide? Did you talk it over with him or what?"

"We were living in this little apartment close to the campus. We sat down to breakfast one morning, and I saw the same absolute misery in his face that I was feeling. Evidently he saw it in mine, too, because he came right out and asked me if I was as unhappy as he was. I was so relieved I laughed out loud. We filed for divorce. I came home with nice memories of a honeymoon in the Bahamas, a new wardrobe totally unsuitable for Polvo, and the knowledge that if I married again it would be to someone who loved not just me, but the same things I did."

"Clay," Fran said softly.

"We're so much alike we might have been born twins."

"I've noticed. It's obvious that you and Clay enjoy each other's company. Thinking back, it's remarkable how little Jake and I have talked during twenty-one years of marriage." She laughed once, a bitter sound. "I married Jake because he played polo, for godsake. I thought it was romantic. Now I want . . . I don't know. Something different. More." She dropped down in the seat and returned to her preoccupation with her thoughts. We passed only one other vehicle, our headlights briefly joining in the dark. The road descended slowly into the wide valley of the river, dropping more sharply after the mining town of Shafter, where the surrounding mountains remain bare, stripped of trees to fuel the wood-burning boilers of the Presidio Mining Company's operation. The mines yielded twenty-five million dollars' worth of silver from seven-hundred-foot-deep shafts before closing in the early forties. Twelve people now lived in the town, including a caretaker for the mine property.

Fran maintained her silence, not even making a complaint when I turned right at Presidio onto Ranch Road 170 and slowed to twenty as we drove the last fifty miles of the river road that rises and falls across one dry arroyo after another like ocean swells.

The porch light of the trading post cast a yellowish

glow over the double front doors and onto the pickup parked close to the steps. The '76 gray Chevy belonged to a street photographer from Mexico who'd showed up two days ago and had been using my parking lot as his place of business, snapping photos of the marine unit that had moved into Polvo to lengthen the road forty-two miles along the river, part of a joint effort that included civilians, the Border Patrol, and the Drug Enforcement Agency.

"I know Clay drives an old pickup but I don't remember it looking that bad. He could at least have it repainted," Fran said indignantly as I drove past the front and around to our private entrance at the back of the building.

I explained about the Mexican photographer, telling her, "I think he sleeps in the front seat." I pulled up close to the back door so I could easily unload Fran's luggage. As I got out, I caught a glimpse of the reflective glow of a pair of round eyes that blinked and vanished just before I cut off the headlights. Phobe had been on the drain board again, playing in the drip of the faucet I needed to repair.

I noted also that Clay's green Ford pickup was gone, meaning someone had needed the vet. Most of his work is with cattle and horses on the big ranches, and the distance adds hours to the work time. My husband wouldn't have it any other way. He is happiest when he's out on the ranches.

I lifted out Fran's two suitcases from behind the seat. On the other side of the truck, she stood staring at the dark, beyond the trailer that is Clay's clinic, and adjoining pens and kennels for sick animals. She seemed to be envisioning the low hills of rock scree, creosote, ocotillo, and clumped grasses that roll away in a seemingly endless horizon of earth colors shading from buff to yellow ocher, sienna to burnt umber.

Fran said, "I remember the first time I saw this place, I thought, my god, someone lives here."

I laughed, the sound silencing the yips and howls of the coyotes somewhere along the river. "That's what I said the first time I saw Houston." The cold night air emphasized the odor of smoke blowing up from wildfires burning out of control in Mexico. The Trans-Pecos had been covered in haze for days.

The three-thousand-square-foot trading post sits on a rise above the green belt of the Rio Grande. The wood-frame building is set higher than ground level, with three wide steps up to the railed porch in front, and a high peaked roof of sheet tin that needs nailing after windstorms. It looks even more isolated than it is, since Polvo is at the end of the road, hidden behind a low mesa of rimrock. I own six hundred and forty acres of desert, bought for the lordly sum of one dollar by my great-grandfather Franco Ricciotti, who built the trading post.

Clay had left the light on in the long, narrow back room that is our living, dining, and kitchen area. I hauled the suitcases up the short flight of stairs to the sleeping loft above our own bedroom and bath, coming back down to find Fran sitting uneasily beside

Phobe on the couch. The bobcat busied herself licking her damp paws dry. Fran tentatively touched her, then stroked her back lightly. I went to the refrigerator for milk. Hot chocolate sounded comforting and right for the occasion. As I added the instant mix to the milk, I surveyed Phobe's bowl. Only a few oily smears. She'd eaten all the portion of the food log, a frozen concoction of horse meat with vitamins and minerals, that I'd chopped up and left for her.

I heated the mugs in the microwave and carried them over to the couch. Because my sister-in-law looked thin and haggard in the lamplight, I started to ask if she'd prefer to forego the hot chocolate and get some sleep. Then I heard Clay's vehicle drive in. Fran said, "I'd rather not mention my problem."

I nodded my head, not telling her that Clay had speculated that she had husband trouble. We waited, but after Clay's pickup door slammed shut, I heard the crunch of gravel as he walked across the parking area to the clinic. Meanwhile, my sister-in-law drank her chocolate and seemed to relax. I offered to fix something to eat, but Fran said the generous portions at the Reata had filled her up. It was ten minutes before Clay came in and welcomed his sister. I knew right away that he'd changed clothes, and his hair was damp from the shower in his office. The call must have been for a wounded or injured animal and he'd changed because his work clothes were bloodied or soiled. That wasn't unusual, but the expression on his face was.

Fran didn't seem to notice, but I could tell that Clay was seriously worried.

"Hey, girls," he said lightly, catching my eye with a cautioning glance, "were the Marfa Lights showing tonight?"

"Right on time," I said, "and Fran was impressed." I offered to fix a mug of chocolate for him, but he said he had a report to write up that couldn't be delayed and he wanted us to know he'd be in the office for a while and not to wait up.

I nodded at his back as he left and wondered whether we had a case of rabies. We'd had a serious outbreak four years ago, but the state-financed airdrops of vaccine-loaded bait had slowed the epidemic to a crawl, finally reducing the disease to the random animal. However, rabies was never vanquished, and in spite of seasonal rains the year before, drought conditions hung on. Dry weather stress always increased sickness among animals.

Fran said she was tired. I showed her the loft and the tiny bathroom, left a light by the couch for Clay, and went to our bedroom, Phobe padding along behind me. She leaped onto the bed. I showered, toweled off, pulled my sleep shirt on over my head, eased Phobe to the middle of the bed, and climbed in beside her, idly turning the pages of a magazine until Clay came in. While he brushed his teeth, I asked no questions, waiting until he was in bed.

No sooner had he slipped under the covers when he said, "I've been at the seven sisters' ranch. Hattie called me. She had three cows off their feed. I found lesions on the mouths of all three, and around the hooves of one, plus some of the others are looking droopy."

"But that sounds like. . . . It can't be. Can it?"

"I'm praying not. There hasn't been a case of hoof and mouth disease in this country since nineteen twenty-nine. Most likely it's one of the other versicular diseases, but only the lab tests are determinative. I called the Texas Animal Health Commission from the ranch. Tomorrow, I'll call Plum Island and tell them I'm sending blood and tissue samples. Worst case scenario or only bad, we've got a quarantine situation on our hands." He snapped out the light on his side. I turned out mine and dropped my head back onto the pillow. I had intended to tell Clay about the road dancers to amuse him. Nothing would do that now. Plum Island was an idyllic name for the Animal Disease Center, where scientists studied deadly and highly contagious diseases.

I woke from a sleep so deep I was disoriented as to time and place. I stretched my hand out and felt Clay beside me in bed. He moved slightly at my touch but didn't wake. I raised up and looked over his shoulder at the glowing red digits of the clock on his bedside table. Twenty minutes after midnight. The silence was absolute, except for the distant drip of the leaking faucet in the kitchen.

The storm broke with a full-blown chorus of noises.

Wind rattled the glass in the front windows, the suction from the draft under the front doors slammed shut the hall door into our private quarters. Outside, there was a crash and the clatter of something tumbling over and over. The garbage can, I thought. Clay, startled into half-consciousness, jumped from the bed waving his arms like some badass karate black belt and bellowing, "What the hell was that?" I put on the bedside lamp. Phobe burrowed her head under the pillows as the next thunderclap and lightning bang hit, followed by one after another, each one louder than the last. Leaving it to Clay to comfort Phobe, I hurried in the dark to the front to make sure the front doors were secure. The wood frames rattled in the wind, but the lock held. I peered out at the unexpected storm. There sat the gray Chevy truck. While I debated whether to ask the man if he wanted to take shelter in the storage shed out back, lightning illuminated the night. What I saw beyond the parking lot barely registered on my retinas in the blink of the bright flash. A long roll of thunder like drums in a parade, then another flash and the surreal image came again, a kneeling figure in the middle of the road, head bowed in prayer. Some madman, I thought wildly, as I fitted the impression of what I had seen into a growing sense of what the reality might be. I spun around and ran back to the counter where I kept my flashlight and my revolver. I heard Clay calling to me from the hall, but I didn't stop to answer. Pistol in one hand, flashlight in the other, I stepped out into wind that whipped my hair back from my face. Scattered drops of cold rain fell with more velocity than volume. I crossed the parking lot, shining the light well ahead to the huddled figure in the road.

The Mexican photographer had died squatting on the ground, his thick body collapsing down upon itself, chin slumped against his chest, arms hanging limply at his sides, the hands resting against the ground.

Behind me the porch light came on, and I heard the thuds of running feet, and then Clay stopped beside me.

"Dead?" was all he asked.

"Dead," I answered. "Look at his left hand."

Clay bent forward to where I focused the light. "Bloody hell."

I moved the flashlight's beam to the man's head. "They stuffed the finger in his mouth."

THREE

No," I repeated, "I didn't see anyone else. The killer could have been standing right there in the darkness, I suppose, but the sight of that man . . . it looked like something from a horror movie. It scared me, but I had a hard time believing it was real."

Sheriff Skeeter Tate looked as tired as I felt and every year of his age plus ten. He'd been on his feet almost since his arrival, and his unassuming manner and mild voice convinced me that here was a quiet man who might get things done.

He wasn't alone. Deputy Rano Johnson, driving the department's Dodge 4x4, had reached the scene first. The contrast between the two men was remarkable, the more so because it was said they worked well together. Tate exuded competence, Johnson exuded confidence. Some called it cockiness. Tate tolerated the deputy's attitude, it was said, because no one knew the shadows of *la frontera* and the shadings of border life better than Johnson.

Of average height, Tate had gray hair that matched his gray-blue eyes, and both reflected experience and intelligence. His skin was fair and, despite his age, unlined except for permanent creases above the bridge of his rounded nose. The rest of his features were small, eyes and mouth barely marking a slightly lopsided face.

Johnson was several inches taller and thirty years younger, his Mexican heritage showing in his black hair and honeyed skin, his Anglo heritage reflected in eyes the color of a sun-faded summer sky. He had high cheekbones, a square face, and full lips that most women would have envied.

Father Jack had come, too, as soon as he had heard, the urgency of his arrival displayed in the white undershirt showing at the collar of the down jacket he wore over it. Nor had he taken time to put on his boots, but had slipped his size-fourteen feet into moccasins.

We stood grouped around the front counter of the trading post. We'd been here, it seemed, for hours, though in reality the sheriff and Johnson had been the ones up most of the night. Fran hadn't wakened until I went to get her after the sheriff arrived. Clay and I had napped on the couch from four to six. It was now eight o'clock in the morning.

Giving in to his fatigue, the sheriff turned away from the counter and sat down at the table by the propane heater and took a long swallow of hot coffee. "Whoever shot him probably made him kneel down first and held the gun right up to his chest."

"Or the poor man was begging for his life," Father Jack said, shaking his head sadly. The sheriff and Johnson exchanged glances at that, and I knew why.

"Sheriff," I said, "I've read about killings in Juarez like this . . . the finger cut off and put in the mouth. Do you think this was done for the same reason?"

"Five killings. The drug lords are killing anyone who threatens to name names to the authorities. The chopped-off finger is left to make it clear to everyone what happens to snitches."

"*Rata*," Johnson said.

"What?" Tate said.

"The Spanish for 'snitch.' *Poner rata.* He snitched someone off, this photographer."

Tate moved his eyes back to me. "This photographer, what was his name again?"

"Barrilito," I said. "When he introduced himself that's the only name he gave."

"This Barrilito must have been ready to point the finger at somebody, so he was killed." He looked me in the eye. "You sure none of you heard the shot, heard a vehicle driving away?"

"I'm sure," I said. Clay and Fran shook their heads.

"Well, there are silencers for guns. Drug lords usually don't worry about silence, but there's always a first." He had other questions. Were there any people in Polvo that showed unusual interest in the photographer, met with him often, paid more than a few dollars for photos?

My answer, that I hadn't noticed anything in particular, didn't help him, and neither Clay nor Fran could offer anything.

The sheriff looked at Johnson. "Barrilito. What kind of a name is that, anyway?"

Rano said, "It's a nickname. It means 'little barrel' in Spanish. 'Cause of the way he was built, thick-chested and short. Nicknames are big with us Mexicans. *Rano* means 'frog.' "

"You don't look like one," Father Jack said.

"I thought Rano was your real name," the sheriff said, frowning. "What is your real name?"

Rano gave a half smile. "*San Benito de Nuestra Señora del Sagrado Corazón de Jesús*. Saint Benedict of Our Lady of the Sacred Heart of Jesus."

The sheriff said, "And the Johnson?"

"Mama crossed the river."

"I'll stick with Rano," the sheriff said before turning back to me. "What do you know about this Barrilito?"

"Except that he came from Ojinaga, nothing. I don't even know his real name."

Johnson said, "His papers in his wallet show his name was Vicente Soto. We didn't find much in his pickup, except his photographic equipment. Real antique stuff, that. Probably worth some money to a collector."

"The marines have pictures of him, if you need one. They took as many pictures of him with their cameras as he did of them. They thought he was a colorful character."

The sheriff said, "Johnson will stay until the tow truck gets here for the pickup. I'll be in touch."

The sheriff left, and the deputy went to wait in his vehicle. Clay went to deliver iodine solution and copper sulfate spray for the Spivey cattle. The animals had to be doctored daily. I had customers waiting, so I opened for business. Father Jack went home. Fran took a book on Mexico from my shelves and sat by the fire in the rocking chair to read. We had all gone back to our routines, and the only memorial to the photographer's death was the yellow crime scene tape and the stained earth.

Clay returned in time for a late lunch. We ate scrambled eggs on toast. Fran washed up and went back to her reading. I took my place behind the counter. By closing time, everyone from Polvo had been in to hear the details of the murder. I tried to keep quiet about the business of the finger, but the detail was already out and being speculated on. I didn't like it that my name was, no doubt, included in my neighbors' speculation. I knew what the gossips would be saying: Is Texana getting rich the quick way, they would be asking themselves.

Drug smuggling along the border is endemic. *La*

Maldición, the people call it. The Curse. At the major border entry points, like El Paso-Juarez, literally tons at a time, hidden in places such as propane trucks, moved from Mexico into the United States. In our area, small-time smugglers moving less than five pounds at a time were more the norm. The isolated car you pass on the ranch road may have a kilo of cocaine taped under the bumper; the man who asks for directions may have three or four plastic-wrapped bags of black tar heroin in his backpack; the family wading the river may have their Styrofoam ice chest filled with marijuana. The monetary reward in moving even relatively small amounts had corrupted more than one respectable *fronterizo.*

Yet we went right on with our lives, as people do, clinging to normality even when it sometimes seemed as if the corruption and violence were the norm, peace and quiet the aberration. We shopped, went to work, took the kids to school, kept the family together, got on with our lives, because we knew that to do otherwise would be to give in, and thus give up. If we did that, the borderland would empty of all save the bad guys.

We have a saying around here: "My daddy didn't raise no quitter." It fit the people of Polvo, who'd built a community where few would choose to live, in conditions of climate and inconvenience few would elect to put up with. But our lives were enriched by being bicultural and bilingual, something not forced upon us, but lived naturally. Most of the time, the drug culture washed over us, like the flash floods brought by the rains, an inconvenience of a few minutes time, and then things returned to normal.

That's how I looked at Barrilito's murder. Things would be back to normal soon. The sheriff would be stymied, searching for a killer who in all probability had gone immediately back to the other side. In the meantime, I intended to get on with my life.

FOUR

I woke the next morning with Barrilito's murder on my mind, little knowing that disaster would soon be at my door.

Two hours before the first red line of dawn touched the horizon, Clay was up, dressed, and cooking breakfast so he could be in Marfa when the UPS drop opened in order to ship the tissue and blood samples he'd taken from the Spiveys' cattle. Clay served not only as the unofficial, meaning unpaid, vet for the county, but acted as a veterinary service inspector for the USDA under its Animal Health Division, which meant he felt doubly conscientious about his responsibilities.

Fran hadn't come down when I finished putting the

dishes away at five-thirty, too early to open the trading post. I poured myself a second cup of coffee, and sat reading Presidio's weekly newspaper, *The International*.

The big story was the U.S. Immigration and Naturalization Service's decision to enforce an old law that had been ignored. Taxi drivers from Ojinaga could no longer pick up fares in Presidio. Sounded reasonable, but not for those Mexicans crossing over to shop. The walk across the bridge was a good mile-and-a-half, which meant a hardship for the Mexicans. They were now limited to buying only what they could carry on the long walk home. The INS said the Ojinaga taxi drivers, if allowed to pick up passengers in Presidio, violated U.S. immigration law because foreign nationals may not work in this country. Does government know how to solve problems or what? Illegal immigrants by the hundreds of thousands coming across the United States borders with both Mexico and Canada, and the INS cracks down on a few hardworking taxi drivers from Ojinaga while wounding both border towns' economies. In other bad news for *fronterizos*, the federal government had stopped the INS from issuing border-crossing cards to Mexicans seeking legal entry. Now, Ojinagans and others wanting to enter the U.S. would have to make an arduous journey all the way to Juarez to the U.S. consular office. Making life in north Mexico more hazardous, the fires south of Chihuahua were out of control. The Mexican military had been pulled out, leaving the villagers and people on the isolated ranchos to fight the flames alone or flee for their lives.

The good news in the paper was the opening of the bicycle plant in Ojinaga that would employ several hundred people. Those items took me through the last drop of coffee. With five minutes until opening time, I scanned the remainder of the headlines. A man stung to death by killer bees as he crossed the bridge. A father and son arrested by the Mexican border officials for bringing a handgun into Mexico. The pair had to be tourists. No local would be so foolish. Mexico takes its gun laws very seriously. I glanced at the clock. Time.

I never open early because we *fronterizos* like ritual, mine being the dependability of my opening and closing hours. In Mexico and the borderland, living life is as important as making a living. Thus during the rest of the day I may be out, and my customers will wait patiently or come back another time, with no hard feelings or indignation. I checked the Seth Thomas wall clock that I had inherited from my maternal grandmother, then went through the short hall that divides our private quarters from the front business, down the aisle between merchandise shelves, and opened the doors.

Three marines dressed in camouflage, their boots laced tight, the bills of their caps lined up with their eyebrows, stood waiting by a Humvee.

"We'd like to get a few things, ma'am," Lance Corporal Lang said. He glanced over his shoulder toward

Mexico. "The smoke is getting worse. We've had orders to be ready to pull out in case the fire jumps the river."

"As low as the river is now, the fire could roll right across," I said. The drought conditions had left the Rio Grande looking more like a series of *tinajas,* potholes that catch rain or runoff, than a river. "A wildfire five or six years ago destroyed eight houses in Polvo. I've been lucky the trading post has never been damaged." I held the door open as I spoke, welcoming them in. Two weeks ago a parade of Humvees, bulldozers, front-end loaders, maintainers, and dump trucks had rolled by the trading post. Since the marines had arrived I'd sold more beer, magazines, snacks, film, and candy than I normally sold in a month, maybe two. And my video rentals had quadrupled. Besides "ma'aming" me to death, the marines had devoted some of their off-hours to climbing onto the roof to fill a hole from a gunshot, killed two rattlesnakes taking the afternoon sun on the warm gravel of the parking lot, and jump-started Glafiro Paredes's worn-out pickup four times. Their community relations included taking every kid in Polvo for a ride in a Humvee.

Their job, cutting a new road bed through the hard rock bluffs known locally as the Presa, was anything but easy. The present lava-rock track was fit only for four-wheel drive vehicles driven by the bold of heart and the strong of arm. Those with a real need to get there could drive five miles upstream, provided the single lane was not blocked by rock slides or washed out by flood. The big ranches dependent on the track for access assumed the responsibility for keeping it open. Because of an increase in drug trafficking, the DEA and the Border Patrol wanted the road improved and extended so they could monitor jennie runners—illegals—and mules—drug runners—too often one and the same these days. The sound of powerful diesel motors had disrupted our quiet days and disrupted the teaching at the one-room school as the slow work of road building went on.

Phobe's acute hearing had picked up the marines' voices. She sidled into the front room, her golden, round eyes fixed on one of the young men. She stalked him stealthily as he moved between the aisles. When he bent over to reach for something on a lower shelf, she sprang, landing on his back. He stayed down and still, looking over his shoulder and telling his friends, "Somebody get a picture of this, will you?" Phobe cooperated, staying on his back until the picture was taken. The other two paid for chips, dip, and magazines, while the one rubbed Phobe's belly as she rolled on her back on the floor. She yowled in disappointment as they left.

A short time later, Fran came out asking if she could borrow my pickup to go into Presidio. "I want to look around that new gift shop you told me about," she said, my keys already in her hand. I didn't think she was so much interested in the gift shop as in avoiding further conversation about her husband problem. Fine with me. I didn't mind listening, but I wanted Clay to be on hand when she asked, "What should I do?" That way, nothing I said could be held against me. She'd forgive her brother saying the wrong thing, but not a sister-in-law. Life had taught me that people who say they want advice mostly don't.

Morning business was brisk after that, with locals coming in for groceries and gas. Used tires are my best-sellers, but occasionally I move a big-ticket item, the odd air compressor for instance. Steak-night sales, we call them.

Clay returned around ten, saying that from Marfa he had seen the smoke from the fire in Mexico, which wasn't surprising. Earlier in the year, we'd choked on acrid haze from fires as far away as central Mexico. Now we had one at our back door. Clay loaded supplies into his mobile vet clinic, the "vetmobile," as we referred to it, a vehicle we'd gone into debt to equip with state-of-the-art diagnostic and surgical equipment.

"Need anything from Presidio?" he asked, ready to leave again. On most Fridays Clay took his practice to his customers in Presidio. Borderlanders are hardy and they expect their animals to be. Pets are rarely vaccinated or neutered. Clay hoped to change such attitudes. Progress was slow, but he was nothing if not persistent and patient. I told him I didn't need anything, and he was out the door.

The first call came half an hour later. The concern in Lucy's voice carried even over the telephone line. "Texana, have you looked outside lately?"

I told Lucy to hold on and I'd look. Lucy Ramos is our postmistress, a nice neighbor and not one to worry or give alarm unnecessarily. I didn't run to the porch, but I walked fast. Over the drooping gray-green of the salt cedars that have smothered the riverbanks on both sides, I saw what looked like a line of low, thick rain clouds rolling up from Mexico, except that the clouds were too low, rising from the ground and thinning as they billowed skyward, and the smoke we'd been smelling for days looked thicker. I listened for the telltale crackling sound of brush burning, heard nothing, and went back to the telephone.

"It's fire, Lucy. Coming this way, but not close enough to hear yet. I won't ring the bell now, but I think we should start notifying people. Be sure to remind everyone to round up their animals."

No sooner had we hung up and the telephone rang again. It was Gwen Masters. From the site of her house on the rimrock she had an unobstructed view of our stretch of the river. "Honey, we've got us a fire going on the other side. It looks from here like it's coming right for you folks. Better get ready to move out fast."

I didn't ask her how much time we had. Fire moving across desert scrub moves swiftly, and the rain the night before had come and gone so fast that it had been immeasurable, doing nothing to dampen the dried-out, frost-killed grasses and brush. I hung up, got my call list from the drawer, and dialed the first number. I had five ranches on my list, all families living beyond the road's end. Lucy, who had one of the few telephones in Polvo, had six. For those close by I would sound the alert by ringing my great-grandfather Franco Ricciotti's two-mile iron bell hanging by the well house out back. Ten tolls meant prepare to leave. Any more meant get out fast. The volunteer firefighters from Presidio would come when and if we needed them. The ranchos and villages on the other side would fight the fire line with feet, shovels, and burlap bags—all they had. In the meantime, I rang the bell ten times, one reverberating note after another, so loud the sound came back off the canyon walls in a double echo. After that, all we could do was watch, wait, and hope.

The air smelled of camphor from the burning creosote bushes. Beyond the trading post, the sky, the river, and the far side of the road had vanished, engulfed by the white smoke of burning grass and brush rolling toward me. Shadows moved in the smoke. Singly and in groups, dark figures emerged like three-dimensional ghosts, Mexicans on foot fleeing the other side. Children held hands, keeping together. A man carried a young child on his shoulders. Some of the women carried babies, others precious household items, family pictures, pottery, or baskets of clothes. One had a chair tied to her back. Silently and steadily, they passed by the trading post and moved up over the low hills. Not only humans, but wildlife fled the flames. I saw snakes slithering for their lives, four coyotes, a gray fox, and the bigger blurred shapes of running deer, natural enemies joined in a bolt for safety.

In the time I stood there, the Coke bottle thermometer tacked to the wall climbed steadily upward from the season's normal daytime temperature of seventy-two degrees to ninety-nine degrees. And still the wind blew from the south, pushing the smoke and fire out of Mexico and toward us, forcing me inside. I closed the windows and put on the ceiling fans before going out back. I took firm hold on the thick bell rope and knelled out twenty strokes. Inside, I gathered into one bag our most precious possessions, a portrait of my parents, Clay's grandfather's Colt .41, the turquoise jewelry that had been my mother's, plus a change of clothes for Clay and me. I carried the suitcase to Clay's pickup, made sure I had the keys in my pocket, and went back inside to coax Phobe to the kitchen. I chopped part of a food log and left her to eat, hoping she'd feel sleepy on a full stomach. While she smacked her food loudly, I went to the utility room for the large dog-size carrier we use on the rare occasions we have to transport the twenty-five-pound bobcat.

I heard a noise out front and went to see what it was. An antique John Deere tractor pulling a rusty, once-red trailer had parked, motor running, in front of the trading post close to the door. Pete Rosales, old school friend and near neighbor from the other side, sat astride the tractor. Zeferina, Pete's wife, sat on a chair in the trailer. She held Meatball, a Chihuahua, on her lap, surrounded by assorted mutts, bawling goats, fourteen children stair-stepped from toddler to teenager, and one thin and wiry old gentleman named Glafiro Paredes, known as The Letter Man, because he delivered mail from the post office at Polvo to Mexicans across the river. Everyone talked at once, trying to tell me about the fire. Glafiro greeted me with a gold-toothed smile, saying over the insistent voices of the children that Pete had picked him up on the way. Glafiro's pickup was worn out and seldom in running order. I reached through the bars of the trailer's sides to scratch Gringo the pit bull on his head.

Pete hushed the others, wiped his hands on his jeans, and said, "There's nothing between the store and the fire but God and river. We got out just ahead of it," he said. "Our place is probably burning by now. Of course the goats have eaten everything for three hundred yards down to the nubs, so we might save the house and maybe the school bus. I'd sure hate to lose that bus. We just built in bunk beds for the grandkids. I heard your bell ringing so I guess you guys are ready to go. I've got everything live from my place in the trailer."

"Clay is already in Presidio. All I have to do is load up Phobe, and I'll be right behind you."

"Be sure you are," Pete said, turning to look at the school bus from Polvo as it sped by filled with kids and followed by three pickups loaded with desks and books.

Pete pulled out, perhaps inched is a better word. The tractor moved at twenty-five miles an hour, tops.

I didn't wait for them to drive out of sight, but hurried to hit the three-inch red emergency cutoff button mounted on a pole near the gasoline and diesel pumps. This cut off the flow from the two above-ground tanks at the far side of the building. Then I moved to the tanks themselves, checking for leaks around the fittings and caps. As I did, I could hear a steady flow of vehicles driving past, headed for safety in Presidio. Finally, I looked over the pumps for leaks, all the while hoping that the fire wouldn't get this far, because I had no idea what might happen to the tanks. I figured the hoses on the pumps would burn, but the cutoff would take care of all but the residual gas in the lines. What I didn't know was how much heat the tanks themselves could take. Until recently, I'd relied on the old underground tanks put in sometime during the forties, so I'd never had to worry about it before. If the tanks blew, the trading post would go with them.

I had started up the steps when the honking began, an irritating *toot, toot, toot*, obviously intended to attract my attention. I turned to see an RV materialize out of the smoke and stop by the pumps. The fat-faced, sweating driver leaned out the window and shouted over the rumble of vehicles going by, "I need to top up my second tank."

"Have you got gas in the first?" I said, knowing that if he had a full tank, he could make not only Presidio, but beyond.

"It's a long way, and I don't intend—"

"My pumps are shut off. I'm trying to get out, too."

"I insist that you cut the pumps on."

"One tank will take you out of my sight, mister. Move on." I spun on my heel and went inside, shutting the door on whatever else he might have to say, but watching through the window to make sure he drove off. As the RV cleared the parking lot and vanished into the smoke, my pickup turned in.

What the hell did Fran think she was doing, coming back here? She must have seen the smoke from Presidio. She opened the driver's door and almost fell getting out. Leaving the motor running and the door wide open, she ran for the porch while the truck's buzzer alarm sounded.

"There's a fire heading this way," she said, gasping for air in the smoke. "I heard about it in Presidio. They say it's bad. They say it may jump the river—"

"Fran, it's okay. We're prepared. I'm ready to leave. Why don't you grab your things and put them in my pickup while I load the bobcat. I'd like to get Clay's pickup out, too."

In her fear she wasn't listening. "You can see the smoke from Presidio," she said, her voice quavering. "Great big clouds of smoke. What is there to burn, for godsake? I thought this was a desert. We've got to get out. Where's Clay?"

"He's already in Presidio. Don't worry. Help is being organized." City-bred Fran, used to spit-and-polished fire trucks that came on call with seemingly limitless water for pumping, would be doubly frightened to know that we manned the hoses ourselves with water from our wells, and that the pumper trucks, from Presidio and maybe Marfa, drew water from stock tanks and the river where they could. I gave Fran the one bit of information that I thought might comfort her. "Texas and federal agencies have helicopters that carry huge water buckets to fight fires. They're probably on their way and will be here before the fire jumps the river."

Fran, seeing that I appeared calm, checked herself with a deep gulping breath and asked what she could do to help.

"Pack, get in the pickup, and drive back to Presidio." She nodded and went down the aisle and into the living quarters. I went out front and cut off the pickup motor but not before making sure Fran had enough gas to get back to Presidio. The gage for the rear tank was on empty. There was no point in my checking the front tank. I always run on that first. I never leave without checking the gas. Fran, unused to our long distances, hadn't given it a thought. Too late to kick myself for not reminding her, and too late to cut the pumps back on and fill up. We'd take Clay's truck. I turned and saw Fran coming down the steps. She must have thrown things into the suitcase, I thought. Then I saw her face and even I felt a jolt of fear.

"What's wrong?"

"Those people," Fran said, pointing behind me. "I passed those people on the road. Why did they turn back?"

I looked behind me, but I knew before I turned it

was Pete. I heard the tractor's motor over the crackle of the fire on the other side, at least I told myself it was still on the other side.

Pete leaped from the tractor and ran toward me. I met him halfway. We were both coughing, our faces red with the heat. "It's jumped the river down the road, a solid wall of smoke and flame. I'm going to try the ranch road up above. You should do the same."

"Get going, then," I told him.

"See ya," he said, turning away. He climbed onto the tractor seat and drove slowly forward, around to the far side of the parking lot. As he headed north, he stood up on the tractor and yelled back to me, "Don't forget extra tires."

"What does he mean by that?" Fran said in my ear.

"Some of the rocks are flints. They'll cut the tires, but we can make it. We'll have to go together in Clay's pickup. It's around back. Go get in. I'll be there in a minute. I've got to get Phobe."

Inside I found Phobe sleeping in her basket beneath the counter. I lifted her gently, put her head first into the carrier, and pushed her rump until she was all the way in. Then I shut the carrier door. The telephone jangled and I hurried to answer. Gwen's hoarse voice shouted down the wire, "You're still there! Get out! It's right on top of you!"

"I'm going," I shouted, dropping the telephone and running for the carrier, then out the back door, groping in the enveloping smoke for Clay's green pickup.

My hand found the pickup and my heart nearly stopped when I opened the door. Fran lay motionless across the seat, her upper body behind the wheel, the cab filled with smoke from the open window. I put down the carrier, ran around to the other side, opened the door, tugged at her feet and then half lifted, half shoved Fran to clear the steering wheel. Back on the driver's side, I pushed up the seat, lifted Phobe's carrier in, climbed behind the wheel, and turned the key. There was a sputter and then nothing. I could hear the rushing sound the fire makes as it consumes the oxygen in a line before it. I tried again, and the engine started. I backed right up to the kennels, stopped, got out, and turned on the water hose and wet my handkerchief to put over Fran's nose and mouth. I looked around. Beyond the trading post lot on all three sides, orange flames glowed through the white smoke, turning the tinderbox-dry scrub into ash that fell around me. I had no way of knowing how far up the hill the flames had advanced, but there could be no driving out now.

I grabbed Fran under the arms, dragged her into the cement shelter of the kennels, and placed the nozzle of the hose right beside her to run onto the floor around her. She made a gasping noise as the cold water hit her, choked, then yanked away the handkerchief. That at least brought her to, but she was still too groggy to function. I pulled her over to the inside corner and propped her shoulders up against the wall so she wouldn't choke if she got sick again. I replaced the wet handkerchief loosely over her mouth and nose and went to get Phobe. Setting her carrier beside Fran, I took off my shirt, soaked it in the running water, and tucked it over the carrier air holes as a filter. I went back one last time to the truck for Fran's suitcase, dumping the contents onto the ground and grabbing a turtleneck that I pulled over my head. I wet down a second shirt and used the sleeves as ties to fasten it around the lower half of my face. I intended to join Fran and Phobe in the kennel. The cement wouldn't burn, nor the gravel of the lot. Our greatest danger was smoke inhalation.

My hand was on the kennel gate when I remembered the gasoline tanks. I ran.

The tanks were clear of the fire, but only because of the graveled lot. What they weren't clear of was the melting heat that increased in intensity as the flames burned the salt cedars and mesquites on our side of the river. Few woods burn as hot as mesquite, and the surrounding heat felt strong enough to melt metal. I could hardly endure it long enough to turn on the second hose near the tanks and aim the nozzle to spray an arching waterfall that sizzled and steamed as it hit the hot air and the heated metal of the tanks. If I couldn't keep them cool enough, we'd blow up: me, Fran, Phobe, trading post, and all.

I could hardly breathe as the flames consumed the oxygen in the air. Yet it seemed that with the hose running, the temperature cooled a few degrees. Then the spray of water fizzled out. I heard a cracking sound followed by a loud snap as the burning utility pole toppled, the flaming wires flying in the air behind it. No electricity meant no pump. No pump meant no water. I dropped the useless hose. My eyes streaming tears from the smoke, my lungs hurting for air, I pulled the shirt from around my mouth. I felt myself hit the gravel and I thought, I failed—I'm sorry, Clay.

The noise in my ears sounded deafening, a roar that seemed to consume me, then a harsh voice saying, "Don't quit on me, lady," as rough hands lifted me to my feet and a strong arm went around my waist. My rescuer and I stumbled across the lot to the back door of the trading post, which he kicked open with his foot. He got me inside and let me fall onto the couch. "You'll have to manage for yourself. I got to get back to the dozer if I'm gonna save your place." I nodded yes. He went, leaving me with the impression of a fair-haired man with the body of a weight lifter squeezed into khaki work clothes. I sat up, shaky but gaining strength with every breath of relatively smoke-free air. I wanted to see what was happening out front. Until I knew it was safe, Phobe and Fran were better off in the kennels. I staggered through the house and to the window. The bulldozer operator aimed the blade straight into the heart of the flames, uprooting burning trees and scrapping them toward the shallow water of the river. In a series of runs he had managed to create a firebreak a little wider than the parking lot, smothering the flames. I finally understood how he'd made it in, creating his own firebreak as he drove. I went to get Fran and Phobe. As I made my way to the kennel, a second bulldozer roared over the low hill, bouncing and skidding downward, pulverizing the rock scree and sending the sand beneath flying up to thicken the smoke. All around the ground smoldered. The thin cover of scrub and grass had been quickly consumed.

Fran sat huddled, face and clothing soot-streaked, trying to breathe through the dried-out handkerchief. I helped her up and got her into the trading post, then went back for Phobe, who once I let her out in the laundry room was in better shape than either of us humans.

I gave Fran some water. Once she stopped coughing, I went outside and watched as time after time the bulldozers smashed into the burning trees like prehistoric creatures on the attack. Shortly, three Blackhawk helicopters passed overhead. Two headed on toward Polvo. The third hovered and dumped water along the road to the left of where the bulldozers worked. A giant hissing sound went up as three hundred and fifty gallons of water hit live flames. The fire slowed, but it was only down, not out.

Fran tugged at my elbow and, over the sound of firefighting equipment and toppling trees, shouted into my ear, "Are we okay?"

I'm not much for hugging by nature, but I hugged my sister-in-law and said, "We are." Fran gave me a tremulous smile.

It would be four more hours before the wildfire had been tamed. By then, ten Border Patrolmen had joined the civilian bulldozer operators, working behind them to put out the hot spots that could flare at any time. Pete and his brood arrived, saying they had waited and watched from the safety of the Dugout Ranch, where the owner had already had his ranch hands at work creating a substantial firebreak. Someone drove down from Polvo to report that the marines had cut a firebreak and those who had stayed, including the animals, were safe. The Marfa volunteers plus many ranch hands were fighting the fire where it crawled up the hill toward the grassy highlands, taking fences out as it went. We watched together as the Blackhawks returned again and again with more water. Clay had left his vetmobile in Presidio, locked in a friend's garage, and hitched a ride with the volunteers. They made it through, putting out the fire where it had jumped the road farther up, dropped Clay off, and went on to Polvo where they were needed most.

By then, I'd gone in to wash my face and help Zeferina and Fran make sandwiches. The bulldozer operators never rested except to drink the now lukewarm soft drinks, since the electricity was out and the well's submersible pump couldn't pull water. Fortunately I had plenty of paper plates and napkins, and for the night, kerosene lamps. We fed the firefighters in turn as they took brief rest from the heat wave that rose out of the glowing ashes of what had been trees.

"What we need is about twenty *cabritos* and a couple of quarts of barbecue sauce," Pete said, taking his break from stamping out hot spots. "We got the charcoal."

Zeferina and I laughed. Fran asked what Pete had said. I'd forgotten that we'd dropped into river Spanish, a hybrid of English and Spanish, a third language that only borderlanders understand. After I translated, Fran took one look out the window at the goats and turned pale.

By five P.M. the bulldozers had shut down and I got to meet my savior. "My friends call me Boots," he told me as we shook hands. "And this is Joe," he added, introducing the other civilian from the road work crew. Boots and Joe ate four sandwiches apiece, and neither seemed to mind the room-temperature beers. I joined Clay on the front porch, where he and several of the firefighters nursed beers while the rest of the men watched the hot spots.

Clay looked at me, got up, went inside, and came back with a generous glass of whiskey. He pulled up a chair, sat me down, and said, "Drink this." I hadn't realized I was trembling until I got off my feet. I told myself it was fatigue, but I knew it was the aftereffect of fear. I drank the whiskey. Clay brought me a thick sandwich and I ate, getting hungrier as I went. When I asked for a second, Clay smiled for the first time since he'd arrived home and said I must be feeling better. The next thing I knew, he was shaking my shoulder. I'd dozed off right there in the chair. A Border Patrol agent came to tell us that some of the firefighters would be on hand most of the night until they had satisfied themselves that the fire was cold. Clay and I both expressed our gratitude, and I made a mental note to send as fat a donation check as I could afford. "Just part of the job," the agent said as he left us to go back to fire tending.

"Pete and Zeferina and their kids will need a place to stay until it's safe for them to go home and see what is left of their property," I told Clay. He proposed the Rosaleses spend the night in the trading post, and we would take Fran and drive to Marfa and spend the night at the Paisano Hotel.

"Why not Presidio?" I asked.

"I checked before I came. The Three Palms Inn is full up. We'll try the Paisano and hope they had a cancellation."

"On the weekend of the Marfa Lights Festival."

"If we have to, we'll drive to Alpine to find a room."

"A clean bed in a hotel sounds great." I stood, stretched stiffened muscles, and went inside to tell Fran and to pack a few more things than I had thrown into the bag for us earlier.

I knew the hotel wouldn't take pets, much less a pet bobcat, so I put Pete's son Alejandro in charge of taking care of Phobe, explaining to him when and how much to feed her. He listened solemnly, promising not to let his brothers and sisters roughhouse with the bobcat, something Clay never allowed since a bobcat can forget a human doesn't consider nips and scratches play.

Zeferina was so grateful to stay in the trading post

that she wanted to start washing the inside walls, where in spite of the closed windows, the pervasive smoke had left streaks. I told her not to bother. I'd hire some extra hands later to do a thorough cleaning. I showed her where the kerosene and lamps sat on the front shelves so she could have plenty of light. I told her to help herself to anything thawing in the freezer and give the rest to the Mexicans left homeless by the fire. Clay and I agreed that the family could stay as long as they needed, depending on what Pete found when he crossed the river again.

I summoned up enough energy to change into clean clothes and we left for Marfa in Clay's pickup.

I had to admit, as I sat next to my sister-in-law, that I was proud of Fran. She wasn't selfish, but she was spoiled, and I hadn't expected her to cope so well and without complaint.

I fell asleep listening to Fran tell Clay about the sad state of her marriage, and thinking that she had been so helpful today, putting up with my yelling orders at her, that she could live with us for while if she wanted to.

FIVE

That's visual shit, that is."

Cobalt blue hair crowned the speaker's head, a golden ring pierced his left nostril, diamond studs adorned his earlobes, and a bright tattoo of a cherub marked his upper shoulder.

I didn't mind that the fashion victim offended my eye, but I did resent his vulgar reference to a painting by my favorite artist, a man in his thirties named Howie Crosswell, who'd married a Marfa woman.

Fran said, "I think I'll buy it."

She and I stood wedged shoulder-to-shoulder in the crowded gallery of the Espuela Foundation's main building, a restored adobe and wood structure that originally had been an army quartermaster's warehouse. The decor was a marriage of Mexico and big ranch country, represented in the courtyard by the giant bronze cast of a spur, the foundation's logo; *espuela* is Spanish for "spur." To better display artworks, the three plastered walls had been color-washed in a soft yellow. The long wooden wall had been stained adobe orange and decorated with a frieze of famous ranch brands. In front of this wall twelve *equipal* tables and painted wooden chairs provided the evening's guests a place to enjoy the bite-size beef and shredded cabbage tacos, squares of jack cheese topped with chunks of avocado on crackers, pico de gallo salsa, and fried tortilla chips. Our local restaurateur, Picasso Beens, had personally prepared the food. Icy-cold bottles of Lone Star beer had guaranteed a steady level of gaiety. The strumming guitars, the violin, and the tinny trumpet of the five strolling mariachis, dressed in silver-studded, black broad-brimmed hats, short fitted jackets, and tight trousers, provided atmosphere to the buzz of conversations that rose over the music.

The soiree was an annual gathering on the second night of the Marfa Lights Festival. Fran and I had come without Clay, who had preferred the street basketball tournament on the courthouse square. Most of the male guests wore cleaned and pressed variations of their work clothes, and were almost evenly divided between jeans and western suits. The women's attire varied as widely as their ages and hair colors: ankle-length or midthigh dresses; low-cut blouses over skin-tight jeans worn with high-heeled boots; and western skirts topped with painted silk blouses and fringed leather vests.

The painting Fran admired had a yellow and brown setting in which the artist had depicted a man driving a wagon. You could almost taste the dust churned up by the horses' hooves and the wagon wheels. It was one painting among a juried display of one hundred pieces by various Trans-Pecos artists working in a variety of mediums. As in most art communities, many called themselves artists, but genuine talent belonged to a handful. Howie Crosswell had plenty of local admirers, but he had yet to gain any critical respect on a wider scale. He'd made most of his sales with locals and by doing commission work, at least when he had first moved here. Lately I hadn't heard much about him.

Fran touched my arm. "Someone's waving at you. It's that couple we saw dancing on the road, with another lady."

I turned to see Ella Spivey, pinned between her older sister Leila and Julian Row, moving in our direction. Though the dress patterns differed slightly, both women wore blue that matched their eyes. Ella's long white hair was swept up, Gibson-girl style, while Leila's shorter, tight curls framed her bony, weathered face in a practical fashion that was the essence of her personality. Row had dropped the western dress for a look that, to my eye, better suited his small stature: gray slacks, a shirt the color of oatmeal, and a cashmere vest in charcoal.

I introduced Fran to the trio.

"We're so glad you're all safe," Ella said, her hand fluttering out in my direction. "Are you getting on comfortably at the Paisano?"

"More than comfortably." I turned to the ladies' escort. "Julian, you were so generous to let us have your suite until the electricity can be restored and the smoke cleanup begins at the trading post. Your kindness turned a near disaster into a holiday weekend for us, besides giving my friends the Rosaleses a refuge."

"Dear Ella suggested that you might need a place to stay after the fire and invited me to the ranch. She's always thinking of others."

I swear I saw Leila Spivey raise an eyebrow. Among sisters there are few illusions.

"Julian is too modest," Ella said. "As soon as he found out you were at the hotel trying to get a room, he telephoned me and suggested you and Clay have his room. I'd already told him about this dreadful problem with the cattle and how helpful Clay had been—"

Her lips in a tight smile, Leila said, "Let's not bore Texana's guest with cattle talk. It's dull for those not in the business."

"Yes, yes," Ella said, her face flushing as she realized she had brought up a subject she shouldn't have. The last thing the Spiveys would want was for word to get out about the possibility of a contagious outbreak before it was confirmed. Leila quickly introduced another topic. "Did you hear what caused the blackout?

Hooliganism. Somebody used a rifle to shoot out the transformer at Rio Grande Electric's substation."

"The sheriff thinks it must've been kids," Ella said.

"A kid who's a crack shot," I said, "or very lucky to hit the exact spot on a transformer to do that kind of damage."

Leila gave a derisive snort. "Most of us Spiveys could shoot that well. Our daddy taught his girls to handle guns as well as horses."

Ella said, "Someone used the opportunity to break into Julian's room. Thank goodness he wasn't there, or he might have been killed."

She leaned her shoulder against his and briefly touched her cheek with her hand. Leila cleared her throat, and Ella's hand dropped back to her side, but the loving look didn't fade. Who was this man, I wondered, and how had he insinuated himself so firmly into Ella's life?

"I was never in danger," Row explained. "I came back from a concert in Vizcaino Park and found my things all over the floor. I suppose whoever the thief was, he'd have gone on to other rooms, except the manager went upstairs to reassure the guests."

"You've probably made Texana nervous about staying there, now," Leila said, her look and voice clearly rebuking Row.

"The theft doesn't worry me," I said. "Something like that is unusual, almost unheard of, in Marfa. I'm sure it was a one-time thing."

"Let's hope so," Leila said.

"I hope you didn't lose anything valuable or irreplaceable," I told Julian.

"Hardly. A little cash. Uncle Sam makes new money every day."

Ella said, "The thief took a pair of cuff links that John Connally had given Julian. He and the governor were personal friends."

"Now, Ella," Row said. "Those cuff links were sent to me after I sponsored a campaign fund-raiser. I'm sure John's people sent them to others, too. John and I weren't buddies, more like acquaintances. He'd call me now and again to talk politics. He liked to keep in touch with lots of people that way. I did go hunting with him a couple of times. He made this one shot on a running buck that was amazing."

Row told the full tale.

"How did you meet the late governor?" Fran asked.

"Oh, that's a long story, and all too sadly in the past, now. As a young man I knocked around the world a bit and was fortunate enough to meet some fine and interesting people."

"Julian once owned an art gallery in New York," Ella said. "He has been educating me in the finer points of art. Tell Texana and Fran what you told me about the sculptures."

Julian demurred, saying to Ella, "You exaggerate my opinion into expertise. Your own taste in art seems impeccable to me. I'm learning from you."

At that moment Noe Myler, a third-generation rancher, spotted Fran and, hooking his arm through hers, got the introduction he appeared to have been coveting. His athletic build and rugged good looks carried his age well. The custom western-cut suit didn't hurt his looks any. In five minutes his courtly behavior had both charmed and amused Fran, and for the first time that evening, my sister-in-law appeared to be genuinely enjoying herself.

Of course, put two or more locals together and the talk soon turns to topics that interest us.

"My ranch is downwind of that damn sewage sludge New York City sends down here every day," Noe said. "The next time I see Ann Richards, I must remember to thank her for dumping on Texas. Sorry for the language, ladies, but our beautiful area is being abused by outsiders and nobody east of the Pecos cares." The veins in his neck swelled as his anger throttled up his blood pressure. "Our Mexican amigos have coal-fired generating plants across from Eagle Pass, belching up god knows how many kinds of pollutants into our skies. And what with the German air force buzzing cattle and busting hearing aids all over the Trans-Pecos, we might as well have targets on our backs. Let 'em train over London like they used to. I swear I don't know what our politicians are thinking."

I said, "They're thinking we don't have enough votes to matter. Here we have one of the last open spaces left on earth, and the politicos are using it for waste disposal. Where will it end?"

"You need to organize," Julian Row said. "I have some lobbying experience, if I can help. Of course, my contacts are somewhat dated, but they could give you an introduction to those in current favor, so to speak." In a short breath, Row name-dropped former Texas politicians Dolph Brisco, Gib Lewis, and Jim Wright into the conversation.

"Mighty nice of you," Noe said, "to want to be helpful."

Ella preened, obviously proud of Row. Leila stared at him as if he were telling tales out of school. Noe was courteous but cool. I happened to know he was a longtime friend of fellow rancher Dolph Brisco. He probably viewed Row's offer as patronizing. The locals had been organized for two years against such abuses of government, to little avail. If the numbers weren't big enough, or the negative publicity great enough, not much stopped the bureaucrats from getting their way. It was scary to know how little control you had over the quality of your lifestyle, over the land you respected and loved and wanted to protect.

Fran's eyes glazed with boredom and her polite smile wavered as Row's voice droned on and on. When Noe took back the conversational handle, the subject flipped to the drought and the economic decline that accompanied it. Finally even Noe wound down, and Ella and Julian excused themselves to attend the street dance soon to begin. As they strolled away, arm in arm, Leila followed three feet back, like a chaperon.

Noe nudged me, saying, "That man is a real *mitotero*."

Mitotero. Literally, myth maker. A big talker, a braggart, someone who enlarged personal reality to include wishful deeds. In Mexico, saying things because you wished they were truth was considered an art. Noe's tone indicated a lack of appreciation for myth-making as an art form.

"I know Ella's soft, but do you think Leila's swallowing that blowhard's line of chat?" said Noe, who'd known the Spivey sisters since their school days together. "I judge him to be a man who lies so much he'd have to ask a neighbor to call his cattle up."

"Maybe what Leila thinks doesn't matter in this case," I said.

"Well it'll be the first time, then." He shook his head, then asked Fran and me if we'd join him at the buffet. I explained we'd promised to meet Clay, and Fran and I were left on our own.

Fran scanned the room. "Tell me about these people."

I took in the room with fresh eyes, noting groupings and names I hadn't given much thought to until Fran asked. "The people standing around the buffet and talking mostly to one another are the third- or fourth-generation progeny of the men and women who founded Marfa and established the ranching industry out here, names that are legend in the history books of the Big Bend and Texas ranching. They're cordial, but they own space, so they demand space from those unlike themselves. In the pecking order, they get the first peck. The tight bunch gathered by that coyote sculpture are the business types who want Marfa to grow even if growth sucks up our most valuable and scarce resource, water. We live in a desert, but the growth crowd can't think past their own pocketbooks to a very thirsty future. Then there is the full western regalia crowd, the ones loaded down in turquoise. They're the incomers from the big cities who have bought parts of the big ranches being broken up or local historic buildings, usually both. Most of the artists are in that group, or at least financed by them. So, Fran, take your pick—longhorn cheese, American, or Brie."

"Texana, you constantly surprise me."

"I'm nothing if not opinionated."

"Who is that striking woman with the long black crimped hair standing next to the big scruffy-looking man?"

"That is Cosmé Vega Crosswell and her husband. You know, the artist whose work you just said you wanted to buy."

A male voice whispered in our ears. "Hard to believe he is the artist and she is a ranch manager, isn't it?" Picasso Beens grinned down at me, not an experience I'm used to, being tall myself. Picasso possesses classic good looks and casual elegance. Clad in chestnut brown slacks, loafers, and a suede shirt in soft yellow, he looked happily at ease and also out of place, yet no one belonged more. Picasso comes from local ranching stock, west Texas born and bred. I introduced him to Fran as the owner of The Nuevo Eatery, a recently opened restaurant in Marfa with a schizophrenic menu that reflected the dichotomy of local taste; for example, grilled blue quail served with red and yellow peppers in olive oil, black bean and tortilla soup, and mango ice with raspberry sauce; and chicken-fried steak with cream gravy, french fries, and chocolate cake with double chocolate icing for dessert.

"The name is the one on my birth certificate, not an affectation," Picasso explained. "The things parents do to innocent children. I would have changed it, but by the time I was old enough, it would have been a waste of all those long years of childhood learning to handle the kidding."

Across the room, a slightly slurred voice bellowed, "You effete little lizard. Who asked your opinion about art. That hair dye has penetrated your brain, if you ever had one."

Conversations ceased and heads turned.

"Your artwork sucks, cowboy," the youth with the blue hair said. "Better stick to painting barns."

Noe Myler stepped between Blue Hair and a furious Howie Crosswell. Howie is as square-jawed and well muscled as something from the cover of a bodice-ripper romance novel, even down to the flowing locks of hair, which in his case come from a simple disinclination to get haircuts.

"I'll paint a barn with you, you ugly peacock!"

Blue Hair should have been grateful for Rano Johnson stepping in to help Noe keep the two apart. Instead, as the deputy moved the young man out of

Howie's extensive reach, Blue Hair yanked his arm away and in doing so elbowed Cosmé Crosswell in her ample chest. I could hear her grunt of pain across the room.

Johnson, his face flushed, regained his grip on Blue Hair, twisting the boy's arms so tightly behind his back the poor kid matched Cosmé's sound of pain with a cry of his own. At the same instant, Howie's fist hit Blue Hair's nose with a stomach-turning smack, and blood spewed.

Fran put her hands over her eyes. "Like being caught between two slamming doors," Picasso said.

A short, stout woman with white hair in a buzz cut and severe black eyebrows that at the moment matched the tight line of her angry mouth, slapped a hand down on the tabletop hard enough to hurt. "That's enough of that," Neva Reiner said. "Rano, you and Cosmé get Howie out of here and leave Jon to me."

As soon as Johnson let go of his arms, the blue-haired Jon felt the spot where his nose had been and slid to the floor. Neva Reiner grabbed a handful of linen napkins from the buffet table and pressed them against Jon's hemorrhaging nose, while instructing someone else to elevate his head so he wouldn't choke on blood, then telling still another person to bring the car around to the back door. Johnson and Cosmé, clutching Howie's elbows, departed out the front.

Fran said, "Artistic temperament?"

"Common imbibing," Picasso said. "Howie has real

talent, but he'll lose it, and his wife, if he's not careful. And the line for Cosmé has been forming for some time."

The small-town sinner has no place to hide. Awareness passed in knowing looks and the gentlest of hints, except when the sin shouted out as with Howie's public drunkenness.

The gallery crowd was thinning rapidly. Two men lifted a whimpering Jon to his feet and half carried him out to the car for the twenty-five-mile drive to the hospital in Alpine. Neva Reiner, who'd managed to attend to Jon without getting blood on either her white silk shirt and pants or her hands, came across to welcome Picasso, be introduced to Fran, and acknowledge me, one of Presidio County's most insignificant merchants. I saw the gleam in her eye as she heard Fran's name and asked whether she was related to the well-known Jake Dare, which Fran acknowledged.

I didn't know Neva well, Marfa being outside my home territory, but she didn't run a foundation with as much money as the Espuela had by lack of knowledge about the state's bigger fish. That Fran was from Houston would have been enough to interest Neva. The Trans-Pecos was becoming moneyed Houston's weekend playground, bringing cash into an otherwise dormant economy.

"Just when the evening was going so well," she said. "I hope, Mrs. Dare, you'll come back and see us again. I'd like to talk with you about our educational outreach to young artists."

"As a matter of fact," Fran said, "I'd like to buy Mr. Crosswell's painting. *The Wagon* is the title."

Neva nodded, a pleased look on her face. "Splendid choice. Please, come this way."

While the business details were conducted, Picasso and I made our way around the gallery. We were admiring a series of black-and-white photographs of the cemetery markers at Shafter when a young woman came and removed Howie's painting from the wall and carried it away.

"Neva's new assistant," Picasso said. "One of the perks of running a foundation is a fair share of wannabes hoping to master the trade. One has to learn the manner and the moves."

Fran came out with Neva at her elbow. She thanked Fran again, and mentioned that her assistant would see the painting delivered safely to the hotel the next morning. We said good night. Neva turned back to the party guests, ready to work another sale, no doubt. Picasso said he'd walk with us to the square. Once outside, Fran decided she needed a jacket, so we left Picasso and started for the Paisano. Halfway there, we ran into Clay.

"We've been to the fights and bought art," I told him, briefly explaining about the fracas between Howie and the art critic, and Fran's purchase.

"I hope you didn't pay much. Have you two eaten?"

"No," Fran said.

"Then let's get our coats and join the music, dancing, and eating going on around the square."

We entered the hotel at the Highland Street entrance. The evening before, draped in soot and smelling of smoke, we had rushed to the suite Julian had turned over to us, eager to get cleaned up and too tired to appreciate the tiled lobby of El Paisano Hotel. I had been inside a few times before, to see the photos of Elizabeth Taylor, Rock Hudson, James Dean, and Chill Wills, taken when Hollywood came to town in 1955 to film *Giant*. It made the community forget the killing ten-year drought that brought starving cattle and monstrous debt to ranchers. However, it was the Spanish baroque-style building I loved, its old-world charm and grandeur now somewhat faded, but still evident in the proportions of the public rooms and grace of the two-story architecture. Fran had been so exhausted she hadn't even asked about the building, but that morning, feeling human again after a good night's sleep, she had commented on how nicely old-fashioned and romantic everything was, from the carved oak bed to the marble-topped dresser. Fresh flowers, courtesy of Julian Row by way of Marfa's only florist, had improved my spirits, and a hot shower and two shampoos to remove the smoke from my hair had done the rest. Since the hotel presently lacked a restaurant, we had gone to Carmen's Cafe for breakfast.

I unlocked the door. Clay immediately checked to be sure he had no messages. Always the worrier, he had called Pete twice earlier in the day. Pete had reported that he was treating all comers to melting ice cream. Fran fetched a sporty-looking wool jacket from the second bedroom, and I changed into a warmer jacket in bright red plaid. Clay waited on us. For warmth, he'd put on a vest over his shirt that left his arms free. He had a half dozen such vests for work out in the cold and wind.

It was a block to the courthouse square, where a band known as the Five Fronterizos played cotton-eyed joes, polkas, and you-name-its for a crowd more enthusiastic than high schoolers at a prom. Picasso Beens stood on the corner, tapping his toe in time to the lively music and watching the dancers. He'd put on a supple-looking leather bomber jacket against the chill. He spotted us coming and waved us over. Many of the crowd were out-of-towners, but I immediately noticed Ella Spivey and Julian Row moving gracefully alongside the county judge and her husband and the banker and his wife. The city secretary and the saddle shop owner danced by and the mayor whirled Leila Spivey around more or less in time to the music. Gwen Masters's partner moved like an oil-well pump jack, but Gwen grinned at me as if enjoying herself. The tourists danced with holiday abandon.

The musicians broke long enough for the dancers to change partners, then struck up a waltz tempo. Picasso asked Fran to dance. Clay took my arm as if to join them, but my hunger won out. "What is there to eat?"

"Frito pie, taquitos, pizza, corney dogs, and quiche."

"Taquitos." We strolled the square, the courthouse

blazing with lights, until we located the right food stall and ordered. The taquitos came wrapped in waxed paper and we ate as we walked until we found spaces on a bench, where Ella and Leila Spivey sat at the other end, both nibbling at something folded in a napkin. I swallowed the last of my food and asked if any of the other sisters had come into town for the festival.

Leila said, "No, not with . . . things at the ranch so busy just now. Also, Viola is feeling under the weather."

"You must try one of these *buñuelos*," Ella said, holding up the napkin. "They're fried while you wait."

The band took a longer break. Fran and Picasso strolled over, talking and laughing together. Clay stood up to make room for Fran to sit. Leila and Ella and I sqeezed together to make extra room. Julian Row appeared, balancing before him a molded paper holder with three deep, plastic cups.

"Here we are ladies, margaritas. Made with fresh lime juice, tequila, and Triple Sec, just like they prepare them south of the border." Leila and Ella relieved him of two. "Reminds me of a little restaurant I often visited on a charming side street in San Miguel de Allende. The proprietor had a big handlebar mustache and an expression as fierce as a bandit, but he was an educated man and a splendid cook. The odd thing was that he always closed on weekends and holidays. Do you know what he said when I asked him why? He said too many people dined out on holidays and weekends and it made too much work for him, so he closed. That man was a philosopher."

Ella laughed, Leila looked as if she'd heard the story before, and Picasso appeared to be thinking about something else altogether.

"Julian has been everywhere," Ella said. "He has done what I always wanted to do, travel the world. My, how I envy the life he has lived."

The emotion behind her words made me wonder what tales the *mitotero* had been spinning privately in her ear.

"I'm going to travel right now," the subject of her admiring eyes and envious words said, "and fetch margaritas for the rest of you. My treat. Ella, dear, will you hold mine?" He handed her his glass and hurried off.

Leila said, "Ella, I think we should get *buñuelos* for everyone. Will you go, dear? I'll hold Julian's drink until you get back."

"Of course," her sister said, getting to her feet. "Here. Oh, you already got one cup. I'll just sit this one here beside you and you can take—"

"Sit them both down, Ella, and go, or we'll be finished with the drinks before the food." Her tone was sharp, her eyes unsympathetic.

Ella did as she was told, as I imagined she always had. While we waited, Leila put down her own cup and fished in her purse for money, saying she was sure Ella had none with her. "She's so scatterbrained."

Picasso asked Fran if she'd seen the Marfa lights.

When she said she had, he told her a favorite local story. "During the Second World War the army built an airfield and flying school near where the lights appear. Of course, the soldiers noticed them almost every night. The men got so curious they decided to use the training planes to pinpoint the exact location of the lights, but every pilot that went up said the lights kept moving and seemed to speed up or fade the closer the plane got to them."

"Hasn't anyone tried simply walking toward them?" Fran asked.

"You bet. A phalanx of Sul Ross students mounted a huge dragnet of the whole area, with Jeeps on the ground and a plane in the air. They saw the lights and tried to walk right up to them. Afterward, the kids said the lights moved like a coyote or panther being trailed, never following a straight path, circling back, and finally vanishing. Taking evasive action. Spooky, I call it."

"Intriguing," Fran said. "I'm surprised Marfa isn't overwhelmed with those people who believe in space aliens. Surely someone must have come up with that as a cause."

There was some confusion when Julian returned as we shifted around to try and make room for everyone on the bench. Leila insisted that Julian take her place beside Ella, who in spite of Leila's prediction returned with a paper bag full of cinnamon-sprinkled *buñuelos*. Finally we arranged ourselves, with Picasso and Clay standing. Leila, who had commandeered the container that held the cups from Julian when he sat down, passed out the drinks.

"You were right, this is good," Picasso told Julian.

We sipped the margaritas. Later, Julian asked Fran to dance and soon we were all dancing. At one point, flushed even in the cool fall air, I retreated to the sidelines to watch and found myself next to Lizzie Bailey, owner of the ranch neighboring the Spiveys. The genial widow nodded toward Ella and Julian as they danced by, and in a stage whisper said, "Who'd have thought it, after all these years that Ella would get her a man. Trouble was she didn't want to marry a rancher, and out here . . . she used to say to me, 'Lizzie, where ever am I going to meet anyone? The only place we go is to cattle auctions.' The trouble with the Spivey girls was their daddy. He was a proud man. He brought them up to think their stride was a little faster than everybody else's. They fairly worshiped him, though he did wear his temper like spurs. It was always his way or nothing. To my mind Leila's the same, just waiting to boil over if you cross her."

"I don't know that I've ever seen that side of Leila, but then I don't really know the Spiveys that well."

"And hope you don't. When we were kids together she bullied us all, but not nearly so much as she did Ella and most of the other sisters. Even Viola, the oldest, used to give in to her. She just wore them down with pure mule-headedness. Their daddy brought them up to know everything about ranching, and Leila knew the most. Those girls roped, worked cattle, and mended fence. Even though everybody says old man Spivey had hired help even during the Great Depression. And after the Big Dry of the fifties, he was the first to restock his land with cattle, when everybody else was near to starving from ten years of that drought. I think he's the reason none of those girls married. The way he brought them up, they didn't need a man around. The twins and Leila thrived on the life, and I think the others liked it well enough. Clara and Ella weren't cut out for it. Those two took after their mother's people. Softer. *Fragile* is the word I'd use. Ella used to cry when her daddy would take her out of school to help work cattle in the fall. When she got a little older she put up such a fuss he left her alone. I never thought she'd stay on after he died, but by that time she was a grown woman and then some. I guess she thought it was too late. I'm glad to see her enjoying herself a little. This fellow, whoever he is, has been good for her."

Mrs. Bailey said the last with a hopeful hint in her voice that I might be as forthcoming about what I knew of Julian Row as she had been about the Spiveys. I couldn't oblige because all I knew, or at least believed, was his name.

As soon as Mrs. Bailey realized I had no information to share, she turned her attentions elsewhere. I lost track of time, but my first hint that something was wrong came as Clay and I danced a third time.

"Tripping the light fantastic!" Clay said in a giddy voice. He laughed and laughed and whirled me faster and faster until I spun out of his grip and fell to the ground.

"That man's drunk," I heard someone say. Clay shouted about diamonds sparkling. Picasso came and helped me get him to the bench. He gripped our hands and wouldn't let go. "Where am I?" he asked.

"Clay, what's happening to you?" I said. Was he having a stroke? Around us the dancers whirled and the band played, a festive background at odds with a personal crisis.

"Too bright, too bright. Moving too fast," Clay cried in a voice I didn't recognize as my husband's.

"Let's get him back to the hotel," Picasso said.

We helped Clay rise and he bolted, darting like a football halfback through the crowd, miraculously not knocking anyone down. Picasso ran after him and I ran after Picasso. Clay vanished into the courthouse, Picasso close behind him. By the time I reached the hallway, I could hear two sets of heavy footsteps thumping up the wooden stairs. I went up the first flight of steps two at a time, but still the pair stayed ahead of me. I followed the sounds of thudding feet and gasping breath past the high-ceilinged courtroom, up and up, grasping the balustrade to pull myself forward faster, the circular stairs narrowing as we moved up to the third floor. At the fourth, a straight flight led to the cupola, normally locked but left open on this night for the festival visitors.

Clay stood in the middle of the dome-shaped room, the lights from the square shining thinly through the series of long windows. Clay stared at something only he could see. Picasso stood close by.

"The stars are so bright," Clay said. "I feel as if I could do anything. I think I must be drunk." He vomited explosively. His body folded. Picasso leaped forward, grabbed his shoulders, and kept him from collapsing.

Feet sounded on the stairs and Julian, followed by a man I didn't know, came into the cupola. The stranger looked at Clay, limp and weeping, and said, "Can't hold his drink? Better get him home."

Picasso said, "Shut up and help me get him downstairs."

They carried him down the stairs. Julian Row took my elbow and escorted me downstairs, saying kindly, "He'll be just fine. You'll see. Poor dear."

Fran was waiting outside. We got Clay into the back of someone's Land Rover. I never found out whose it was. I got in beside Clay, supporting his head and shoulders against mine.

SIX

Fran said, "Texana, I think he's awake."

I jerked up in the chair beside the bed, my body stiff from the all-night vigil we'd kept. Clay opened his bloodshot eyes, focused them slowly at the dawn light coming through the gauzy curtains, and said, "Who poisoned me?"

I wondered whether I looked as pale and sick to him as he did to me. I bent over him and squeezed his hand so hard he cried, "Ouch."

"You realized it then?" I said.

"I thought I was joking, but it's not funny. My brain is mush."

"It's no joke. You really were drugged, but. . . . You scared me badly, you know."

He lifted my hand to his lips and kissed it.

"Could you eat something?" I asked him.

"Actually, I'd like to brush my teeth and take a shower."

Later, over breakfast brought in by Fran from Carmen's Cafe, I explained.

"Picasso thought maybe someone slipped you some kind of drug."

"This is crazy. I'm not Timothy Leary. I didn't take anything, not even an aspirin."

"No one thinks you took it voluntarily, Clay," Fran said.

"*No one* being you and Texana."

I said, "It was the janitor here at the hotel who suggested it might have been peyote. He helped Picasso and me get you to bed. He said you acted like the gringos who came to his hometown to take peyote for a religious experience."

Clay said, "If that was a religious experience it wasn't sent from God. I saw cold blue lights and then I was moving through colors like gemstones. I felt like I was drowning. My chest hurt and I couldn't breathe. I was sure I was going to die. What made the janitor think of peyote?"

"He is Rarámuri."

"He should know, I guess."

The Rarámuri Indians live among the deep gorges, high peaks, and dusty plateaus of the Sierra Madre Occidental, the Mother Mountains of the West, in Mexico. They keep to themselves, or try to, and to the old way of life. The Mexicans call them the *cimma-rónes*, the wild ones. Peyote is a part of the Rarámuri religious life. Shamans dig the waxy, blue-green cacti from the coarse, bleached earth with ceremonial chants, later taking it under carefully prescribed circumstances and in exact amounts. It contains mescaline, a hallucinogenic.

Clay rubbed his fingers across his head. "I feel as if I'd run a marathon carrying a sack of cement. How obvious was my condition last night?"

"People were dancing, the music was loud, and the few who noticed you running into the courthouse probably thought you ate a bad taco."

Clay looked distressed.

"Folks will assume you had too much to drink. You weren't the only one."

"Is this Rarámuri still around? Can I talk to him?"

"I'll find out." I called the manager, who told me he would locate the janitor and send him to our room.

Calisto Rivas was a stocky, round-faced man of indeterminate age, with skin the color of rust and thick black hair cropped low across his forehead and shaggy in back. He was dressed in a white shirt over a white T-shirt. His new jeans were much too long for him, so that the legs creased and folded from the knees down, dragging in back against the heels of his tennis shoes. He took a seat at the table across from Clay, sitting calmly erect.

"Calisto," I said, "is from Cusárare. He was educated by the Jesuit fathers at Creel. He has a married sister living here in Marfa."

"Leaving home takes courage," Clay said to him.

"Life in Cusárare was once *tranquila*, but the world is moving in on us. The forest is gone, the old habits are dying, and the men who come say we must plant poppies. When I refused, they tried to kill me, so I left. *Así es la vida*," he said. That is life.

What was a little drug-induced nightmare compared to being run off your own land by drug lords, I thought.

"Señor Rivas," Clay said, "I wish you well, and more important, I wish someday that you will be able to return home and take back your own land. My wife tells me I owe you thanks for explaining what was wrong with me last night. Now I need your help again. I didn't take peyote, so it must have been given to me. Is it easily mixed in food or drink?"

"You can chew Old Man Peyote whole. The shamans take him when he is fresh and the spirit powerful. For others, the shamans give Old Man Peyote ground up to a fine powder and put in maize beer. In Creel, there were two witches who gave peyote ceremonies to outsiders. Only a fool acts like a shaman without a shaman's wisdom. The Peyote People may help or hurt those who use them. When I saw you talking and weeping in your sleep, I knew that you were communicating with the Peyote People. I feared for your greatest soul, that they might take it. If you have more dreams, you must find a shaman to give a peyote ceremony to save your other souls."

Clay said, "You're a wise man, a man of experience. I'm grateful for your help."

Rivas stood. *"Iwérasa."* When Clay shook his head, Rivas struggled with the translation, saying finally, "Be strong."

Clay shook his hand and I showed him to the door. I asked Clay whether he felt well enough to go home.

"Is the hotel manager eager to be rid of me? Not that I'd blame him under the circumstances."

"Father Jack left a message with the manager for us last night." I read from the slip of paper I'd been keeping in my pocket: *Electricity back on. Things here are getting out of hand. Nothing to worry about, but I think you should come home.*

"That tells me a lot. Let's go."

Fran said she'd be staying. She had a dinner date with Picasso. I glanced at Clay to see what he made of that. His face was beaded with sweat. I asked if he wanted to wait a few hours, but he shook his head. I collected our things and we left, wondering what we'd find at home.

SEVEN

Is Pete holding a fire sale?" Clay said.

I had geared myself up for the shock by daylight of the full aftereffects of the fire: the scorched earth, the charred tree stumps, and the deep scars left by the blades of the bulldozers, but nothing could have prepared me for the sight at the trading post.

The first warning had come a mile before we reached home. At first, we thought perhaps the pick-ups and cars parked along both sides of the road belonged to Mexicans from across the river who'd been burned out.

A quarter mile from home trucks, cars, a bus, and even a few burros blocked the road, forcing us to park and walk. In front of the trading post, vehicles filled the lot, the road, and the ground all the way to the river. The side lot was solid with humanity, standing, kneeling, sitting in lawn chairs, on boxes, and makeshift benches of sawhorses and boards. Marines in sunglasses and fatigues stood on the front porch watching the crowd with all their attention focused on the southeast wall of the trading post. As we got closer we heard the babble of voices and many in the crowd swayed raised arms in time to chanting. Everyone in Polvo seemed to be there.

"It's Lucy," Clay said, his tone as astonished as I felt. I checked my watch. Ten o'clock, a full two hours before she closed the post office for the day. In all the years I had known her, Lucy had never shut the doors early.

Father Jack, his face dismal, appeared on the porch and motioned us over.

"Do you see that," Clay said. "He's dressed in his clericals and it's not Sunday. It must be the Second Coming."

"Or someone died."

"He'd still be in jeans and a golf shirt."

We started a slow push through the crowd. Clay held my hand to keep me from falling as I tried to step over a kneeling woman. Someone called my name.

I looked around to see Claudia Reyes. A rapt expression on her face, she said, "*Mira*!" Look. She pointed toward the trading post. "*Nuestra Señora.*"

Our Lady. I looked, but all I saw was smoke-streaked wood. Claudia was saying something more, but she had turned away from me and I couldn't hear. A stir, like ripples on water, moved out from Claudia and through the crowd. Those in front of us blocking our way began to move and shift, clearing a path for us. As we passed, one woman, cradling an infant in her arms, tugged first at Clay's hand and then mine, crying out, "You are blessed, you are blessed!"

We reached the front steps.

Father Jack Raff, all six foot, four inches of him, red beard shining in the bright sun, shouted over the general noise, "Welcome home! Just in time, too. You can see why I said you'd better come home. You have to see it to believe it."

"What the hell is going on here, Jack," Clay said.

"Let's go inside."

We walked past the marines, who obviously found the crowd entertaining.

"Is Pete still here? Is everything else okay?" I asked, looking around inside anxiously.

"Hey," Pete said, coming down the aisle and grabbing my hand to shake it. "Am I glad to see you. We need more candles, snacks, sodas, bottled water. Lots of stuff. I got a list somewhere. Too bad you don't sell rosaries."

"Are you bragging or complaining, Pete," I asked.

He grinned wider, obviously enjoying himself. Father Jack said, "You're still on duty, Pete. I'm going to talk with Clay and Texana."

"Gotcha, Padre." Pete turned to me and added, "Phobe is in the utility room in her basket. Zeferina has the kids out back in the kennels sitting with the dogs. Otherwise they bark and bark at all these strangers."

We went to the back and sat around the kitchen table. Faces of the crowd clustered at the windows, staring in at us.

"I'm closing the damn curtains," Clay said. He blocked out our audience, then turned back to the priest. "What started all this?"

Father Jack, his solid bulk overflowing the chair, his wide arms packed tight into the long, black sleeves of his jacket, spit out two words like a curse: "Andromeda Zavarias."

"What about her?"

"She came to get groceries for old Rosa and fell down on her knees in the parking lot, shrieking that she saw Our Lady on the wall. There must have been half a dozen people here when she pulled the stunt and within ten minutes we had twenty. They haven't stopped coming since. I'll have to let the bishop know before he sees it on the news."

"This is going to make TV news!" Clay almost shouted. "That's all we need. There must be three, no, four hundred people outside. If it hits the news, there'll be who knows how many. This is a store and a veterinary clinic, not a damn sideshow for the media to come and snicker at like a—"

"Easy man." Father Jack was on his feet, his hand clamped on Clay's shoulder. "I didn't mean the media had been here, but in case they come, I have to notify His Excellency first."

"I don't like this," Clay said.

"Nor do I. It's embarrassing to the Church. We promote the faith, not smoke and water apparitions."

"Does the smoke stain or whatever it is really look like an image of Our Lady?" I asked.

"If you have a vivid imagination you can see some sort of shape, I guess," Father Jack said, "but I don't care if you can see the color of the eyes. This is hysteria, not faith. And it will spread. The silly girl is bragging that *Nuestra Señora* is giving her messages and promising a great revelation in the days to come. Our Lady doesn't manifest herself on walls and never to a person like Andromeda Zavarias. If Our Lady appears, she reveals herself to the innocent and the quiet. Andromeda has never been quiet and, for all her youth, has long since ceased being an innocent." He looked more upset than I have ever seen him.

"So, what are we supposed to do?" I asked. "If I scrub the image into a bucket of soapsuds what will happen?"

The priest pressed his fingertips together and shook his head. "I believe those poor souls out there will think you're committing an act of desecration."

Zeferina stood in the doorway, waiting to be noticed. I went to greet her. She asked if she could prepare some food for us. For the first time, I noticed the house. Zeferina had dusted, polished, and waxed everything that needed attention. All traces of the smoke inside had vanished along with cobwebs in high corners and dust bunnies under the furniture.

"I should be cooking for you," I told her. "This place looks new. I'll bet you washed Phobe, too."

She didn't laugh, but acknowledged both the joke and the compliment with her shy smile.

"We'll make do with whatever is ready. Don't worry about us," I said. She nodded and closed the door.

"Why don't we call the sheriff," Clay was saying as I sat back down. "Maybe he could persuade these people to clear out. At least send a deputy down here to see that the road stays open so the school bus can get through without running over someone kneeling on the road to worship Our Lady of the Trading Post."

"That might make things worse. We don't want to make people mad. Tate hasn't been here all that long. He doesn't know the river as well as he does Marfa," I said, thinking wistfully of Andalon, my old school friend and the former sheriff. He'd have known how to handle this. But Andalon, due to his pivotal involvement in clearing up a smuggling ring, had been asked to join the DEA, and was now posted in El Paso. We were still learning Tate, who according to his campaign ads had been in the military police before becoming chief deputy in Cass County. He'd retired and relocated to Marfa, just in time to run unopposed in the special election held the previous year.

Clay leaned in close to Father Jack. "Can't you get

them to go home? Tell them to. You're a priest. Surely seminary training covers this—this—"

Father Jack said, "I've tried to get the crowd to go home, pray there. I might as well be mute as far as their hearing me in this matter. They aren't listening. Try the sheriff. We're going to need him anyway, as you said, to keep the road open. He should be informed. If you call him, I'll handle the bishop."

"Tell the bishop to be useful and come down here and put a stop to this nonsense, since you can't do it," Clay said.

Father Jack looked around at me. I couldn't explain how rocky Clay was already feeling before he'd come home to this. So I tried running interference. "Pete did mention how good it is for sales—" I closed my mouth after the look Clay gave me.

Father Jack grew short-tempered himself. "I'm not wearing my blacks because it's stylish or comfortable. I put them on for the authority of the costume. I blessed the crowd with holy water, gave a righteous prayer, and asked them to go home and keep the image of the Virgin in their hearts. For every person that left, three more showed up. If the Holy Father himself were here to ask them, I doubt that crowd would disperse."

"So you're saying—"

"I'm sorry, but for now, you've got a shrine on your hands." He marched out.

"You were a little hard on him," I said.

"I can't believe there's nothing he can do."

"We could call the Holy See. Request the Pope to make a recording for us. Test Father Jack's theory."

No laugh, but a twitch of Clay's lips, then a sheepish, "I'll apologize to Father Jack next time we see him, or make a hell of a donation."

"We're going to spend all night keeping an eye on those burning candles out there to be sure one doesn't set the building on fire. You'd think they'd have seen enough flames."

Clay said, "No, we're not. I'll get Ruben Reyes and a couple of other reliable men to keep watch over our flock by night. We'll call the sheriff in the morning. He's going to love having to come this far twice within a few days. We've probably single-handedly doubled his crime statistics for Polvo."

Zeferina fed us so well we felt like guests in our own home. She had prepared stacked, homemade corn tortillas layered with green chilies, onions, asadero cheese, and a spicy sauce. Clay opened Carta Blanca beer for Pete, himself, and me. Zeferina drank water and the kids had Cokes. We allowed Phobe and one dog, Gringo the pit bull, to sit under the table. Gringo curled up at Pete's feet. Phobe stayed close to mine, rubbing her head against my legs and taking an occasional swat at the dog, an old friend and playmate of hers.

Zeferina and I washed dishes while three of the children dried and stacked. Pete offered to stay all night and help keep an eye on the pilgrims, but we knew he was as anxious as Zeferina to get home and find what the fire had left them. We loaded them down with blankets, an oil stove, a portable propane heater, lanterns, and food and they left, the tractor and trailer making a ceremonious exit through the crowd and along the riverbank, with goats bleating, kids waving, and dogs barking. The marines were gone, too, the novelty apparently worn off.

I locked the front doors and turned the sign to CLOSED. Turning in early, Clay and I made up to Phobe for our being away by brushing her fur an extra long time as we all three curled up in bed together, the two human companions drinking a short whiskey to numb frazzled nerves. We could hear the sonorous hum of prayers from outside and beyond, from somewhere near the river, a radio tuned to an Ojinaga radio station.

"What do you remember about last night," I asked Clay. "You must have been given the peyote either in the food or in the drink."

"I have no idea."

"The taquitos were in individual servings, but the fillings would have been in common bowls. Someone could have dropped in peyote ground up or powdered, if that's what it was—"

"We can't be sure what I was given. And we haven't a clue who or why. Leila handed out the drinks. I remember that much."

"Julian Row went and got them. He was sweet to me when we were getting you to the car. Kept patting me and telling me how everything was going to be all right. I think he was really shocked about what happened."

Clay only frowned, keeping silent for so long I finally said, "What is it? What are you thinking?"

"I'm thinking that after Leila handed me a drink, I passed it to Julian, who was sitting by Ella. When I turned back, Leila was passing a cup to Picasso. I helped myself to the last one except hers."

"You're saying it was Leila Spivey who spiked the drink?" I said incredulously. "There *was* all that fumbling in her purse when she thought Ella might have left without money. And she did have three drinks beside her on the bench then. I suppose she could have put something in one. But why?"

"Your friend Julian could have put something in one of the drinks before he brought them back."

"He isn't my friend. I just said he was kind to me."

"I wish I could remember if Leila noticed when I gave the drink she handed me to Row."

"And I, for one, can hardly wait for you to check the cattle again tomorrow. It will be interesting to see Julian Row at home with the Spivey sisters." I turned out the bedside lamp, snuggled down under the covers, then sat up immediately and snapped the light on.

"What now?" Clay said.

I jotted on a notepad I keep by the bed. "I've got to double order beef jerky tomorrow. Sales are booming at our friendly, neighborhood shrine. And no more references to those 'people.' We call them pilgrims from now on."

Clay groaned. "Give it a rest, hon."

I turned off the light. "Good night."

"Night."

EIGHT

Tate said, "You have a real dilemma here."

"We had to clear the road as we drove." Ever vigilant, Deputy Rano Johnson's eyes scanned the room as if memorizing it.

We were seated at the table by the window overlooking the desert beyond the trading post. In the sky ten or eleven vultures rode the warm air currents. The graceful, airborne scavengers kept their heads cocked sideways, keeping an eye on the burned expanse far below for the carcasses of the small and large creatures that failed to outrun the fire.

Clay came in from the clinic, where he'd been catching up on his paperwork and hoping to hear from Plum Island. He'd promised me he'd wait to visit the seven sisters' ranch until I could go with him, an acknowledgment of his awareness of the possible after-effects of the drug.

"I'll leave Rano to keep an eye on things," Tate told us. "Normally, Deputy Dennis Bustamente, since he works out of Presidio, would be here to help, but he's working on some heavy equipment thefts. Three ranches have had bulldozers stolen the past couple of months. Half a dozen others have had break-ins."

"Yeah," Clay said. "I heard about it from several people in Marfa. Big market across the river for that sort of thing."

Tate looked at him speculatively. "Speaking of Marfa, I heard you had some trouble there last night. Anything you'd care to tell me?"

"Just a bad reaction to something I ate or drank."

"Sounds like a health department problem." Tate smiled, his teeth crowded and crooked in his narrow mouth. He scratched the back of his neck. "I guess you've given some thought to scrubbing off the smoke stain."

I explained what Father Jack thought about that.

"Well, we'll do the best we can for you. We can't keep it up forever. Maybe this phenomenon will wear off on its own."

"Lot of nonsense," Rano said in his deep voice.

Tate stood up and placed his hat on his head.

"I'll show you out, Sheriff," I said.

The helicopter noise, which had been building as we talked, reached a crescendo as we got to the porch.

Sound travels far in the desert and the river valley captures sound waves between the rimrock on either side. By the time we stepped outside, the Blackhawk, heading upstream, roared directly overhead and only fifty feet above the ground. We turned our heads away as the rotor wash sent dirt and ash debris swirling like someone shaking a giant vacuum cleaner bag.

The sheriff took off his Stetson and shook grit from the brim. "Must have a flare-up of the fire farther out." He looked around at the blackened ground, bare all the way to the river. "You were lucky not to be burned out." Tate clamped a hand on the deputy's shoulder. "Give me a call if you run into overtime." He replaced his hat, said good-bye, and walked to his patrol car.

Johnson settled down on the porch. I went back inside, followed by three customers. The sales rung up, I checked on Clay, still sitting at the kitchen table. "Are you waiting on me?"

"I'm ready to go when you are. I think I'll let you do the driving."

"Why didn't you tell Tate about the peyote?"

"We don't know for sure what it was."

"You'd rather he thought you were drunk?"

"I'd rather let it go."

The seven sisters' ranch lies at the end of a nearly impassable track lined with sotol, Spanish dagger, and other thorny things. At the gate, Leila and Hattie, dressed alike in pants and flannel shirts, helped Pitt Calloway, their ranch hand, hang a new steel gate between two heavy and thick posts with densely rusted hardware.

"Our daddy brought those posts all the way up from Mexico by mule train, along with whole cottonwood logs for the *vigas* of the house," Leila said.

"They've heard that story before," Hattie said.

"We're old," Leila said. "The best stories in our lives are—"

"—behind us," Hattie said.

Pitt glanced at us and nearly smiled. The ranch hand was medium in all things, color, manner, voice, and size. He dressed like the working cowhand he was. A well-washed shirt, jeans tucked into a pair of boots, old but well cared for, and spurs. His wide face was almost as rough as his calloused hands and he looked older than his age, somewhere near fifty. He'd grown up on the ranch and spent his whole life working for the sisters, as his father had worked for their father, Randall Spivey. It was said that Pitt rarely went beyond the barbed-wire borders of the ranch, finding in the land all the world he desired.

We hoisted the gate into place. "Come on and have a look at the cattle," Hattie said. "They seem to be holding their own, but they're dropping weight by the day. Won't be worth hauling charges—"

"—if they come out alive," Leila said.

Friends and neighbors called this habit of finishing each other's sentences sister-speak. The Spivey women had lived together all their long lives. This lifetime of genetic and learned similarities meant that they shared thought processes. They were singular personalities forged into a whole.

A small helicopter whirred by overhead, flying low toward the ranch house.

Leila followed it with her eyes.

"Company?" Clay asked.

"Nope. That's Julian—"

"—showing off for Ella," Hattie said.

"He rented the helicopter from that Houston man who bought the Two Pair Ranch," Leila said.

Clay asked, "Where'd Julian get his flight training?"

"Says he owned a ranch in California and used a helicopter out there," Leila said. "Me, now, I rode out with the hands from the time I was big enough to sit a horse. Our daddy wouldn't hold with ranching by helicopter."

Hattie said, "It was a grand childhood we had. I don't get ahorseback much anymore, but there was a time when I fairly lived in the saddle. Leila's going to have to give it up sooner than she thinks. Getting stiff—"

"—as a plank," Leila said. "We've talked enough. Let's get going."

Hattie drove their blue Chevrolet pickup with her sister riding beside her. Pitt rode on the tailgate. We'd gone a couple of miles when Hattie stopped within sight of a nearby windmill pumping water into a concrete water reservoir. Three vultures, wings spread to catch the sun, perched on the rim. I saw Leila raise a rifle, aim it out the window, heard the loud shot, and watched as one vulture fell. The other two made an awkward takeoff, wings pumping to lift their heavy bodies. Another shot, and a second vulture dipped and hit the ground. The last vulture caught an updraft, rose, and escaped. Leila lowered the rifle and the pickup moved forward again.

"That's one practice I wish their Daddy Spivey hadn't taught his girls," Clay said. "I've tried to convince the sisters that vultures don't contaminate stock tanks any more than the cattle themselves do, but they won't go against their father's teaching."

The basic entrance gate led everyone who came to the ranch to expect a similarly utilitarian house. First-time visitors expressed surprise at the elaborate two-story hacienda that Randall Spivey had built for his bride, Florence Doran. Past the house, outbuildings in various stages of repair and upkeep doted the grassy, treeless landscape: the barn held feed, branding irons, cracked saddles, even an old buggy, the history of ranch life; a bunkhouse that could hold ten hands provided Pitt Calloway with ample room.

Leila and Hattie took us to the stock pens where sixteen head of cattle had been corralled to prevent them from infecting the main herd and wildlife.

The bunched cattle stood with lowered heads and hunched shoulders, their tails hanging limply between their hind legs. More than half drooled heavily, while several had frothy slobber. Clay pointed them out to me, saying, "That indicates the mouth ulcers had ruptured into open lesions. Makes eating nearly impossible. The same type of blisters around the hooves means it hurts to walk." He looked at Leila and Hattie, "Are they eating?"

Leila, as if to prove she could, climbed to sit on the top rail of the corral. "A bit, except for the bull—"

"—he's not eating at all that we can tell. We're feeding alfalfa cubes, all spread over clean hay in the feed bins. We scrape it clean every evening and morning. It fairly kills us to have to burn the leftover feed everyday, but we're doing it," Hattie said.

"And Pitt has been swabbing their mouths and spraying their feet every day like you told him to, but—"

"—it would be cheaper to put the animals down."

"Let's wait and see how things go before we even consider that," Clay said.

Leila said, "Our daddy never gave up on an animal as long as it could hold up its head. We aren't going against what he would have done. I'll never forget the time he hauled feed and water for twenty-seven days to a first-calf heifer with paralyzed hind quarters from birthing an outsize calf. Everybody else said he should sell her for dog food. That cow must have lost two hundred pounds before she finally got up. Turned into one of our best mother cows ever."

"I wish I'd known your father," Clay said.

"I've never met his equal," Leila said proudly.

Clay went over to where Pitt had been standing quietly, waiting, and said, "Let's see if we can get the bull into the squeeze chute with some of the cows and I'll dose him with antibiotic and force-feed him a solution to get his electrolytes up."

Both men put on disposable gloves and rubber boots before entering the pens, slowly moving within close range of the cattle, forcing them to turn and move toward the chute and head gate, a pincerlike device for working them.

"He hasn't heard yet, has he?" Leila said to me, watching with anxious eyes as Clay and Pitt ran the first animal into the head gate.

Hattie said, "From that laboratory."

"Not yet," I said.

Leila shouted a command to Pitt, then said, "Thought not. He'd have said. How's he feeling after the other night in Marfa?"

"No lasting damage."

Hattie said, "Must have been an allergic reaction or some bad food like—"

"—we got when we were children. Daddy took us to Ojinaga and we all got a very nasty illness from the food that took several years of treatment to clear up," Leila said. She paused, and added, "I think it must have been the meat in that Mexican food he ate at the festival."

"I ate it, too." I watched Leila's face as I spoke, but if she was feeling anything more than concern, I couldn't see it. Nor could I imagine Leila Spivey putting anything into anyone's drink.

After that we watched in silence as Clay and Pitt finished treating the cattle. Afterward, they turned the animals back to join the others in the pen. Both men dipped their boots in a pail of disinfectant and threw the disposable gloves into a burn barrel.

"You've done a good job with the cattle," Clay said to the sisters and Pitt. "You are careful, when you doctor them? People can get this, too, and it makes the flu feel good."

Leila said, "We're being careful. We haven't gone into the south pasture where the main herd is for fear we'll spread this awful stuff. Thank goodness this bunch was isolated in the lone tree pasture. Another week, and we'd have rotated them in together in the lower pasture. That would have been a real disaster."

"I'm still convinced this is most likely vesicular stomatitus," Clay said, propping his foot on the lowest rail, his eyes on the cattle. "Like I told you, it mimics hoof-and-mouth disease, and in cattle only a lab test can tell which is which. The blisters have broken in some of the cows and the lesions are more painful than the blisters, so they'll drop more weight. You may even lose one or two that were on the thin side coming into this. Some of the bred cows may miscarry, but if they can hold out, they ought to start feeling better. The disease runs its course in about fourteen days."

Shaking her head, Leila said, "I never thought time could move so slow at my age."

"How long did you say we've got to keep them quarantined if it's not hoof-and-mouth," Hattie asked.

"Thirty days after the last lesion has healed."

"Lordy, lordy. That's a lot of feed."

Clay explained that he had sent registered letters notifying the neighbors bordering the ranch. "The quarantine extends ten miles beyond the premises. No one can move any stock in or out until I give the okay. I'm sorry this is happening to you."

Hattie said, "We lived through the Big Dry when—"

"—everything on four legs was dying in the pastures," Leila said. "But this is mighty scary. I purely hate to see an animal suffer and our neighbors upset."

I put my arm around her shoulders.

She reached up and patted my hand, then said, "Come on up to the house. We have a late lunch waiting for you."

Randall Spivey had been a fanatic collector, amassing a huge collection of paintings, antiques, pottery, and art objects from Mexico. All this was distributed throughout the living rooms, dining room, passages, and bedrooms of the hacienda. Melon-colored walls provided a background for *talavera* tiles, masks from Guerrero, ceramics from Michoacán, hanging *retablos*, and velvet-covered mahogany furniture piled with pillows covered with woven fabric from Oaxaca. Color overwhelmed the eye, an art museum of Mexico's finest crafts. It would take one person hours to see everything. I loved it, but I would have hated being responsible for the dusting.

Leila called out a "we're in" and got a "here" from the kitchen. We passed through the formal dining room with its polished oval table and leather chairs, the shelf-lined walls filled with blue and green hand-blown glass into a kitchen lifted straight out of the heart of Mexico. Divided by a series of arches into two work areas, preparation and cleanup, there was a table, chairs, storage cabinets, and a breakfast nook big enough for all the sisters. Rows of copper pots hung from the *vigas*, and hand-painted tiles in red, green, yellow, and blue covered work surfaces. Functional pottery and cooking pots of every size covered the walls.

Julian Row as houseguest looked right at home, sitting with Ella at the tiled table as they turned the pages of a photograph album.

Hattie's twin, Mattie, and sister Clara fried steaks one after another in two blackened iron skillets on the built-in gas range. Viola, the eldest, peeled and sliced potatoes, Sarah, the youngest, dropped the slices into hot oil in a deep iron pot, and Mattie scooped the cooked fries onto newspapers to drain.

There was not a sign or sight of anything leafy and green. Meat, potatoes, and biscuits. My kind of meal. I sniffed. Over the scent of hot oil I thought I detected a whiff of peach cobbler. My stomach growled appreciatively. I loved the kitchen with windows running the full length of the back wall. We all took seats around the big table, the places already set for *comida,* midday lunch. Mattie forked steaks onto a platter and passed the food. Row greeted Clay with, "Glad to see you feeling better, my boy." When he asked Pitt if he had changed the hay for the cattle in the pens the ranch hand said, "Done already," and forked a chunk of steak into his mouth, looking at Row as if he'd suggested raw oysters over steak.

Leila commented that working with seven women had taught Pitt to save his words, since he was out-talked seven to one. Row and Clay laughed, and Pitt kept right on chewing, pausing to tap Tabasco sauce onto his steak.

Clay and Pitt both ate two steaks and Row had seconds on the cobbler, made by Ella with canned peaches. Throughout the meal, the houseguest entertained us with stories about his travels, mostly lightly self-deprecating tales in which the joke was always on Row. He laughed at himself as heartily as he intended us to. The sisters ate it up as fast as they did the food, all save Leila, whose level of appreciation never rose above a low-grade smile.

After the meal, the sisters and Row came outside with us to say good-bye. As we got into the pickup, there was a distant rumble, and we all looked to the sky, where quilted clouds layered the upper atmosphere.

"Was that thunder?" Ella said hopefully. "Maybe we'll get some rain. Every drop had missed us so far."

Leila snorted in digust. "That's the last thing we need until the cattle get well. Some of us aren't having to clean up after them every day."

As we drove off, I glanced in the rearview mirror at the receding sight of the hacienda.

"The Spiveys are cattlewomen first and last," Clay said. "They take good care of the place, too."

"Julian Row has certainly made himself at home there," I said. "Do you suppose we'll be invited to a wedding soon?"

"If we are, the sisters can say adios to Pitt."

"You don't mean it. He has never lived anywhere else."

"He will if Row puts his boots under a bed here permanently. Pitt is used to working on his own and bossing extra hands whenever he needs help. He's talky when the sisters aren't around. He says that Julian Row has been selling the sisters on the idea of turning the hacienda into a dude ranch."

"Are they interested?"

"Pitt says that most of them like the idea. Leila and Hattie think it's silly. Row has convinced the others that with his help they could hire full-time help and run the place for profit."

"I'll bet Leila is livid. She didn't say a word to me. Do you suppose Julian has been everywhere and done all the things he claims? In his conversation over lunch, I don't think he left out a country in the world that he hadn't visited."

Clay shrugged. "Who knows. He enjoys spinning a yarn, and for my taste, he's overfamiliar, but that's no crime."

As we made the seventy-eight-mile drive home, we watched the cloud cover thin and vanish. No rain for the seven sisters'. All the way home I thought hard about the sisters, their lives, what Mrs. Bailey had told me. Everything I knew. Leila, and to some extent Hattie, was the heart and soul of the ranch. Keeping alive her father's memory and work seemed the most important thing in her life. Ella, by all accounts—including her own—had been unhappy and dissatisfied. What had their lives really been like all these years? I'd always assumed the sisters had remained unmarried because the shared experiences and memories meant so much more to them than did anything else. It was the land that bound them. Would anything or anyone make them give up the land? If Ella wanted to go, would Leila allow it?

"Do you suppose if any of the sisters had married," I asked Clay, "that they would have been forced to divide the ranch or maybe even sell?"

"No. Daddy wouldn't have liked that," Clay said. "Nobody builds up that much land without wanting it to stay together. I do wonder what happens when the last sister dies."

It was nearly six when we reached home. Rano had worked magic, evidently. The road was clear. In the trading post parking lot food wrappers and empty drink cans discarded by the pilgrims tumbled in the wind. The presence of the deputy, plus the blowing dirt and ash, had driven some of the pilgrims away, but more than thirty remained, their flickering votive candles protected by cupped hands. Beneath the wall, a card table held more candles, vases of paper flowers, prayer petitions weighted down by stones, framed photos of the dead, the sick, or the beloved—anyone in need of prayer and a miracle.

The sheriff's deputy sat in his vehicle nearby, drinking a Coke and eating cheese crackers. We parked in back. Clay went to his office. I went inside and immediately looked for Phobe and found her napping beneath the front counter on her burlap bag bed. Someone rapped on the front door. As soon as I turned the lock, half a dozen customers rushed inside, buying everything from gas to candy bars.

Johnson strolled in to say he managed to keep the road clear only by frequent cruising. He'd radioed the sheriff that he'd be needed here for some time to come. The sheriff had said one of the deputies would be on hand for school bus runs.

Phobe picked that moment to bounce out and rub against the deputy's legs. He bent to stroke her head, and she tried to climb into his lap, snagging her claws in the tight weave of his khakis. I apologized and removed her. "I usually keep her claws trimmed, but so much has been going on, I've forgotten about routine things like that."

Johnson smiled, saying, "No problem. I'm officially off-duty as of six, but I'll stick around a while longer and see if I can discourage the folks from staying all night in your parking lot."

NINE

*C*lay dropped the fork full of scrambled eggs halfway to his mouth. "What now!" he said, as we all got to our feet and started for the door.

The wail had come from outside. As we hurried, I could hear murmurings from the pilgrims, who'd gathered in the dawn, lighting votive candles before the wind came up.

The crowd numbered nearly forty-five, predominantly women, their clothes neat but faded and thin from hard use, their shoes the most obvious giveaway to their poverty, their heads covered by scarves in respect of the Virgin's image they had walked far to pray to.

At the moment they watched not the image, but a

young woman, her head draped in a gold lace mantilla made incongruous by the Aztecos band T-shirt she wore with her jeans and pink tennis shoes. She stood posed with outstretched arms, swaying and mumbling between two older, black-clad women. Andromeda Zavarias had brought her mother and grandmother with her.

Clay took one look and all but shouted, "Can't we have just one normal day for a change? Just one regular, boring day."

Andromeda fell to her knees and raised her arms heavenward. That's when Father Jack strode around the corner, aiming straight for the self-described visionary.

She opened her thin-lipped mouth and raised her eyes toward the image, only to see the priest bending over her. A sound of gasping and shock rippled through the pilgrims. The three Zavarias women were reputed to be *brujas,* witches, who readily put the evil eye on those who opposed them in any way.

Father Jack whispered in her ear.

"*La Madre!*" Andromeda spat out the vulgar curse, got to her feet, yanking the mantilla from her head and flinging it to the ground. She turned her back on the priest and walked rapidly away. Her acolyte relatives gave the man terrified looks, one whisked up the discarded mantilla from the ground, and both scudded along after Andromeda, two humped little missiles of venom.

Father Jack, looking angry and embarrassed, aimed

for the porch, the crowd parting before him like the Red Sea before Moses. As soon as his foot hit the top step, I asked him what he'd said to persuade Andromeda Zavarias to leave without stirring up more trouble over the image.

"I'm sorry to say it was a threat rather than persuasion. I reminded her that the Church has paid the rent on the family's trailer ever since her father left," he whispered. "A well-intentioned but perhaps unwise charity. Someone called to warn me she was coming here this morning to proclaim a message from the Virgin. I couldn't let that wicked girl dupe naive souls who might believe anything she said because she claimed it came from holy inspiration. It was either stop her myself or pray for a bolt of lightning from heaven. I decided the Lord wanted me as His instrument, as being faster than building a storm."

Clay offered him coffee, a mute apology for his outburst on Sunday. After he left, Clay drove off in his pickup on calls. We had yet to drive to Presidio and bring back the vetmobile. There hadn't been time. I started on a cleanup of the litter in the parking lot. Armed with garbage bags, I worked around the praying people. As I tied off a bag, a voice said, "May I help?"

I smiled as I turned. The well-built twenty-year-old man wore a long-sleeved shirt in a pattern of bright blue that set off his brown skin. With eyes so dark they looked black, and black hair cropped short, he was handsome enough to be a male model. Pablo Pacheco reached out a hand for the garbage bag. "May I look through that for treasures?" he asked.

I handed him the bag. He sat cross-legged on the ground, carefully unwound the plastic tie, placed it to one side, and emptied the bag's contents in front of him. His smooth-skinned hands sorted through the mishmash of paper cups, cigarette butts, drink cans, water bottles, and prayer slips. I watched him as he found a broken red pencil with gold lettering, a torn copy of one of Barrilito's photographs of some of the marines, and a pearl button with dangling threads. He looked over each with as much careful attention as a shopper in a department store might examine the bargain china. After a moment, he dropped the items into a drawstring bag clipped to his belt, patting it afterward as if to make sure it was there.

He gave me a happy smile, his teeth gleaming, his expression displaying the innocence of his mind, which would remain for all his life at the mental age of a six- or seven-year-old. All of Polvo watched over Pablo. The younger children played with him as an equal, the teenagers protected him as they did their younger siblings.

"Do you want to look for treasures as we go?" I asked. He nodded eagerly and squatted down to scoop the garbage back into the bag. Pablo's liking for checking out the garbage for treasures originated, quite accidentally, with Clay. The boy never to be a man liked to come and see any animals Clay might be caring for and Clay allowed him to help water and feed them.

One day Pablo had seen a cover photograph of a Texas ranger on an old copy of *Texas Monthly* that Clay had been reading. "That's what I want to be," he had announced, his finger on the picture of the lawman. Clay fished through the trash barrel outside his office where he'd thrown a cut-metal logo that had fallen off a client's Ford Ranger pickup. He showed it to Pablo and told him he'd make a ranger badge for him and true to his word he had. The boy wore it now, pinned to the blue shirt.

I let Pablo wander where he wanted, picking up and over the trash, while I concentrated on the parking lot area. For twenty minutes we worked quietly, then Pablo shouted, "Wow," so loudly the heads of the prayerful pilgrims jerked up. He danced up and down and held up something for me to see.

I went over to see Pablo's treasure. Clutched in his hand, as if he feared he might drop it, was a badge from which he rubbed a crust of dried mud.

"Where did you find it?" I asked, and Pablo knelt down and pointed. I looked at the cut in the hard-packed ground where the badge had been stuck in sideways, no doubt pushed there either by the pilgrims' feet or their vehicles.

"Let's go inside and clean it," I said.

We went in hand in hand. I shifted Phobe from playing in the drip and washed the badge under warm water from the faucet.

"May I keep it?" Pablo said.

"I'm afraid not, Pablo. This treasure belongs to the

deputy sheriff. He must have lost it while he was here helping us. I'll put it away somewhere safe until he comes back and I'll be sure to tell him how you found it. I'm sure he'll be very glad to have it returned."

Pablo accepted this with good grace. I gave him another bag and he returned to his treasure hunt contentedly. I slipped the badge into the cash register where I wouldn't forget to give it to Rano Johnson.

For the next two days, our restored routine pushed the murder of Barrilito and Clay's incident in Marfa to the bottom of my mind as I reveled in the mundane. Customers visited morning and evening to shop and gossip, and the repetition of talk about the fire and the storm and the murder touched the extraordinary events with the mystique of high drama, making them seem, if not less real, less frightening. On Friday the UPS delivery brought a package addressed to Fran, still in Marfa, and likely it seemed to remain there. A fire and a murder seemed to have put her off the trading post. She'd taken the suite at the Paisano, after checking with Julian Row, who'd informed her he'd be staying at the Seven Sisters for the foreseeable future.

Clay returned in time for lunch and to collect from the post office the report from Plum Island. The blood and tissue samples from the cattle showed negative for hoof-and-mouth disease. Clay went in person to tell the Spiveys, saying he'd check the livestock while he was there.

Clay hadn't been gone five minutes when Deputy Sheriff Dennis Bustamente strolled in. Short, amiable, a ceaseless romantic with the ladies, pugnacious toward crime and criminals, he patrols out of Presidio. He came in smiling, helped himself to a package of cinnamon rolls and a carton of milk and sat down at the table by the coffee machine to eat.

After he paid, he told me that the investigation into Barrilito's death was stalled. "Lately we've had an unusual amount of drug activity. Three fifteen-year-olds arrested last week with hollowed-out Nikes, a grandmother from Denton County with enough heroin in her bra to buy a Mercedes, a good-looking woman who called in a bomb threat at the International Bridge so she could avoid the sniffer dogs, then had a blowout that wrecked her car right beside the Customs booth. It's like somebody has got a sign out on the other side: DRUGS FREE FOR TRANSPORTING. The sheriff's thinking this photographer had to be smuggling small amounts of drugs in his trips across the border."

Dennis didn't have to put the rest in words and he wouldn't have anyway, since to say more would be to betray his boss. The man had died on my property, his death a message clearly marked as a drug hit. If anything illegal was going on, the sheriff's thinking would be that I was aware of it, perhaps involved.

"The body has been sent to Lubbock for autopsy," Dennis said as he pocketed his change and departed.

An hour later the sheriff paid me a visit, this one decidedly less friendly. We stood outside on the porch to talk. This time, his questions were targeted. How often did I shop in Ojinaga and where? What about my husband? Did he ever work across the river? Did he have any connection or knowledge of anyone on the other side involved in drug smuggling?

The last question alarmed me because I suspected what motivated it. A couple of years earlier, Clay had done some vet work for a Mexican rancher whom the DEA had identified as a major drug lord. Two agents had approached Clay about spying on the man. They wanted information on drug shipments believed to originate from his ranch. Fearful for our way of life and our lives, Clay had refused, an act that didn't sit well with the agents. We'd come under investigation ourselves. Only the former sheriff's vouching for us had kept us out of immediate trouble. Government files never get shredded, they get passed from agency to agency. Sheriff Tate had been asking questions about us, and someone somewhere had sent him a file in which Clay and Texana Jones were mentioned, how prominently I could only guess. The file and the circumstances of Barrilito's murder were enough to justify the sheriff's questions, but though I knew the man was only doing his job, I resented it. Suspicion had been cast on too many innocent *fronterizos* solely because of where we lived. I tried when I answered not to sound as defensive as I felt.

I told him the truth. Clay had helped Gordon "Ghee" Suarez cull his herd during the height of the drought and arranged to sell some of the best stock to a rancher in Oklahoma. We'd been to Rancho de Sierra Vista one time only. The DEA had told us they suspected him. What they knew or could prove, I had

117

no idea. What I didn't tell the sheriff was about my contact with one of Ghee's henchmen and the debt Ghee had owed me and paid, for saving his daughter's life.

"Let's go over again what happened the night Barrilito died," the sheriff was saying. "What made you go to the door and look out?"

We went over it and he followed up with another question. "Any of the marines hanging around more than—"

We were standing on the front porch of the trading post. The radio in his car crackled into life. A voice blurred with static and broken up by the distance and difficulty of the transmission said something indistinguishable to me except for the words *body* and *Lincoln Flat*. The sheriff responded to the call and with his hand still on the transmitter, backed out of the parking lot fast enough to send gravel flying. Apparently someone more important than Barrilito had died.

I stood there until the rolling cloud of dust from his vehicle had settled back to the ground. It seemed to me that the sheriff was more interested in trying to prove that I was dealing in drugs than in catching Barrilito's killer. The real smugglers would know I wasn't part of the loop. If they hadn't, Clay and I would be dead, too. They wouldn't have stopped with the little photographer. But they could hardly testify in my behalf. Now, if I could find the person Barrilito had snitched to, it would help. It had to be someone in authority: a sheriff, a DEA agent, a Customs agent. Anybody wearing a badge.

TEN

He's dead, he's dead, he's dead!" Ella Spivey, her fists clenched, sat between her sisters Sarah and Clara, their faces pinched with concern and distress.

Clay had called me from the ranch to bring him a new starter for his pickup.

I'd taken note of the sheriff's car parked in front of the house, but I'd driven straight to the pens. Seeing Clay's pickup, but no Clay, I'd returned to the house.

Leila had opened the door with a glass in her hand. Ella's tragic voice was the first thing I heard as I walked in. Leila hastened to reassure me. "Clay is waiting in the bunkhouse with Pitt. All it takes for men to scatter is for a woman to start crying." She came closer to me and whispered, "It's Julian. He's been killed, shot. The sheriff's come just now to tell us. He's in the dining room talking to the others. I'm trying to get Ella to go to bed."

Leila went to her sister, whispered something to her, and held out the glass. Ella turned her head away like a tired child. Little wisps of white hair floated out from her neat coil and drooped around her face, making her look like an elderly waif.

"Drink it," Leila told her.

"I don't want it. I want to know when I can see Julian. I want to bury him here on the ranch . . ." She broke into bubbling sobs.

Leila handed the glass to Clara and said, "See that she drinks it, get her to bed, and stay with her." She moved away from Ella, whispering to me, "She'll be asleep in no time. I put one of my sleeping capsules in it."

I told Leila I'd go and find Clay and we'd be on our way, but she stopped me with her hand on my arm in a surprisingly tight grip. "Stay. I want you here. We're all of us a little deaf. I need a good pair of ears."

Like her sisters, I found it hard to say no to Leila Spivey. I followed her into a big dining room where the others sat around the table, the sheriff at the head. He gave me a look that made me want to recite some incantation to ward off the evil eye, but he said nothing.

Hattie was explaining that Row had taken one of the four ranch trucks to go into Marfa. They hadn't seen him since he left after breakfast at seven.

The sheriff patiently went over how long the sisters had known Row, where they had met him, how he came to be staying with them.

The answers came from multiple voices, the sister-speak more in use than usual. Tate's head moved back and forth as if he was at a tennis match. They had met Row for the first time in late spring at some fund-raiser or other they attended in town. He had expressed an interest in seeing a working ranch. He was staying at the Paisano, he had told them, while looking for a house to buy. After the theft from his room during the blackout, Ella invited him to stay in the tiny guest house that had been their father's retreat.

The questions continued. Had he seemed worried? Did the sisters know of anyone with reason to kill him? Had he made anyone angry? Where had the man come from? Did he have a family? What had brought him to Marfa? Had he actually bought a house?

As far as the sisters were concerned, Row's past was a mystery. They spoke of his travels, the places he'd been, the things he said he had done, but could pinpoint neither dates nor times. After the sheriff's questions wound down, the sisters had some of their own. How had Row died? A bullet in the chest from close up. Where had it happened? On the lower half of the Pinto Canyon Road. Who had found him? A couple saw his pickup pulled off the road and stopped to see if help was needed. Row's body was lying on the ground on the far side. When they got out to take a look they realized he'd been shot. They drove to the closest ranch house and called. "By the time I got there," Tate said, "the ground had been messed up with tracks of the couple and the ambulance crew."

"It must have been robbery," Hattie said.

"No, ma'am," the sheriff said. "He had five hundred dollars in cash in his wallet. But no credit cards, unless he left them here for some reason."

The sisters couldn't say.

The sheriff explained that he'd have to go through Row's things.

Leila said, "The key to the guest house is on the peg by the back door. It's marked. Go straight past the pens and follow the road. You'll see the house."

"Anything else you need to know about the ranch, you can always ask your deputy, Rano Johnson. He worked for us as a part-time ranch hand when he was in high school," Viola told him.

"I want to reassure you ladies that we will find whoever did this," Tate said.

When the back door closed, Leila turned pale as dust and would have fallen from her chair had not Hattie and I caught her. We helped her to her bedroom, a small, square room with blue-striped wallpaper, a single bed with a white coverlet, a small antique desk, and lacy curtains at the windows. She leaned back against the pillows. Viola suggested an ice pack. Hattie told her to bring a hot water bottle.

"I want to talk to Texana alone," Leila told them. "Close the door." She curled a finger at me to come closer.

I sat down on the edge of the bed beside her. Her face had collapsed into a slack mass of wrinkles and lines that her normal vigor kept at bay. Even her eyes had lost their life. Anguish as deep as first love gave her the look of death.

She raised her shaking arm and pointed a trembling finger at the desk in the corner. "There. In the middle drawer underneath some graph paper. Get it and read it."

"Get what, Leila?"

"You'll see. Go on and look."

It was a number of typed pages held with a paper clip. The letterhead of the first page read *Bruckner Investigative Services* with an address in Dallas. It was dated August 20. The cover letter was addressed to Leila and read in part: "We have completed the background check on Julian Row. . . ."

I looked at Leila.

"Read it," she whispered.

I sat down at the desk, turned on the lamp, and read. Viola knocked and brought in the hot water bottle, put it under Leila's feet, and asked if she could take a little hot coffee with "a nip" of something in it. Leila said yes and told Viola to bring me a cup, too. In a few minutes she was back, putting Leila's cup by the bed and fluffing the pillows behind her sister's head. She sat the second cup by my hand on the desk and left. No curiosity about what I was reading or why I was still there in the first place. Did they all know about the report? Or did the sisters' close and long lives together dictate such careful issues of privacy?

I read, so intrigued that I sipped the whiskey-spiked coffee without a thought about driving home.

Julian Row was born in 1935 in Potts, in southeast Texas. From the age of fifteen on, Row was involved in minor scrapes escalating into major violations. He left home at eighteen. By the time he was twenty-four, he had served two years in the Texas prison system for burglary. After that, he apparently learned a lesson of sorts. He stayed away from crime that might end in physical violence, such as burglary, working a number of con games and frauds, under a number of aliases. Legitimately, he'd been a waiter, a chauffeur, a would-be writer, and a car salesman. He married and divorced three times. Each of his wives was older and wealthy. During the course of each marriage he persuaded his wife into giving him large sums of cash to invest. He also bought as much community property as the wife's money could afford. In a pattern that was to emerge later in another fraud, the investments always failed. With the money safely in a bank account under another name, Row became so unpleasant that his wife filed for divorce, netting Row half the community property purchased during the marriage, plus the cash he'd siphoned off. Two of the marriages lasted eighteen months. One, only six. Row was known to be a heavy gambler and quickly ran through whatever assets he had. In each of the marriage schemes he used his real name. In 1989, as "Charlton West," he worked a gas well drilling scam. "West" and an out-of-work geologist used slick brochures and much authentic-looking paperwork to con the greedy and naive. "West's" job was to talk people into $10,000 minimum investments in potential gas wells, securing the drilling rights from landowners for a share of the profits to come when the well was in production. Except there were no profits, and "West" and his partner expected none, since the sites selected had been passed over by reputable geologists. The pair would bring in a rented rig, then bus the investors to see their well. Of course, after a few months, the investors were informed by letter that the well produced water, but no gas, part of the risk of investment. On the rare occasion they did hit gas, the partners shut in the well, told investors it was a dry hole, and later sold the rights to a legitimate company. Through creative bookkeeping on the partners' part, "West" and the geologist made a substantial sum. In 1990 their luck ran out when one of the rigs hit a mixture of natural gas and hydrogen sulfide called "sour gas," which in high concentrations can kill almost instantly. The Texas Railroad Commission, which regulates gas and oil activities, has special regulations for such wells, including monitoring instruments, and required notification of evacuation plans for surrounding communities. The partners failed to provide any of this. The well was located on a three-hundred-and-fifty-acre ranch in Hood County where a young woman lived with her two children. At the time her husband was in Kuwait fighting in the Persian Gulf War. One night the well leaked, killing the family as they slept. "West" disappeared along with all cash assets of the partnership before the bogus company was fined the largest penalty ever assessed under the 1975 safety regulations governing such wells, and before charges of criminally negligent homicide were brought against both partners. The geologist was tried, found guilty, and sentenced to prison.

I skimmed the rest of the report. The gist was that Julian Row, alias Charlton West, had vanished until Leila contacted the firm. I found the last paragraph interesting:

The seriousness of the charge against Row *warrants further investigation by the author-*

ities. While the firm maintains an agreement of confidentiality with all clients, the agency recommends that you contact local authorities with this information. Attached you will find copies of newspaper reports and documents.

I looked over the documents. The newspaper stories carried a picture of a more youthful-looking Julian Row smiling into the camera. One of the wives had supplied it, no doubt.

Leila's eyes met mine as soon as I turned around. I lifted the report in my hand. "Leila, I can see why this is upsetting for you, for all the family, but I don't think you need worry about it being made public. Unless the sheriff finds something in it that helps find out who killed Row, there is no need for anyone to know about the details of his past."

"I'm past caring about that. The man whose family died, I know him. Look at those clippings. It's Howie Crosswell. It was his wife and children who died because of Julian Row."

"Howie?" I said mindlessly. I flipped the pages, read the headline, looked at a photograph taken at a funeral. The camera had closely focused on one man's face, trancelike in numbed grief. It was Howie. I replaced the report in its hiding place beneath the graph paper, rose, and carried the desk chair over to the bed. I pulled it close and sat down, looking Leila in the face, my eyes searching for any hint of what was going on in her head. Why was she telling me all this? Did she expect me to do something? What did she want?

She said, "I like Howie. You probably don't recall, but he worked for us for almost a year when he first moved here, must have been four or five years ago now. Pitt had to have an operation and couldn't do heavy work for a while, so we hired on Howie temporarily. He said he'd been working on a south Texas ranch and came out here on account of his painting when he was given a grant. That's all he offered about his past. He was drinking even then, but never in the day. He did his work fine. He lifted the bottle after dusk, drinking himself to sleep. God knows the man must have had nightmares. I thought after he got tangled up with Cosmé Vega in that whirlwind courtship of theirs that he stopped drinking. I'm sure he did. I don't know what started it up again. I tell you, Julian Row isn't worth it, not for a minute. After what he did, he deserved to die and I don't blame Howie one second for killing him."

"Do you know for a fact that Howie recognized Row as West?"

"He must have. Even though he was overseas when his family died, he'd have read the newspaper stories when he came home. His wife probably had other relatives who would have made sure Howie saw Row's picture. I'll bet the press got it from one of those ex-wives of his. It's not a thing he would forget. He certainly wouldn't forget the face of one of the men responsible."

"No, I suppose not."

Leila's rough old hand reached out and clenched mine. "I want you to warn him, so he can get away. Get his story straight. Do whatever he can to protect himself. Before I have to turn that report over to the sheriff, because it will surely get him arrested. I never said a word to anyone about that report, but Rano will have to tell the sheriff about it. I'm surprised Tate didn't already know about it when he got here."

"Rano? What's he got to do with it?"

"I guess I better explain. I knew Row was a predator as soon as I laid eyes on him. When we were introduced it didn't take him five minutes to peg Ella as the weakest and to cut her out of the herd. That girl's been restless for years. Always pining for what she doesn't have instead of appreciating what she has. Our daddy told me I'd have to look out for Ella or she'd go and make a fool of herself. I doubt he thought she'd leave being this foolish until so late in her life, but age doesn't change what you are, and Ella's a fool."

"Leila, you amaze me."

"Because I know my sister's a fool? Or because I'm not too old to take action? Because that's what I did. As soon as Row started squiring Ella around, I went to Rano Johnson. Asked him if he could investigate Row for me. He said he couldn't, but he'd find somebody who could. A week later, he gave me the name and number of the agency. He even talked to them for me on the telephone, explained what I wanted, a background check, he called it." She paused for breath.

"Will you do it, Texana? Will you warn Howie for me?"

"If he is innocent, that's his best protection."

She raised herself up on her pillows. "I think that's a very naive statement. Don't you watch *60 Minutes*? Innocent men can and do go to jail."

"Why don't you just call him?"

She shook her head and said frantically, "If the sheriff finds out, with that and the report, he might think I don't know what. If he goes after Howie, I don't want to have to tell him any more lies than I have to. I can't lie well. Never could. It's all just too much for me. Please, Texana."

"I'll do what I can."

She nodded, accepting my intentionally vague statement as agreement when I had no idea what I was going to do.

I asked Leila one more question. "At the Marfa Lights Festival, did you put powdered peyote into the drink, intending it for Julian?"

She closed her eyes and said heavily, "I thought if he made a fool of himself in front of Ella she might drop him. I got the drinks mixed, I guess. I didn't know Row hadn't got the right drink until Clay got sick, and then it was too late."

ELEVEN

I left Clay buried under the hood of his pickup replacing the starter. On my way home, I made a detour to see the murder site. Lincoln Flat is sixteen miles above the cutoff to the seven sisters' ranch. I identified the spot easily. In the midst of the scrub and sky, three teenagers standing near a red pickup were the only living creatures except myself.

The two boys and a girl stared at the murder scene. The taller boy greeted me by saying, "You come to see where that man died, this is it."

I walked over and joined them at the edge of the dirt road. Crime scene tape tied to stakes driven into the ground wreathed the spot where the body had been found.

"I heard he was shot right in the heart," the girl said.

The taller boy walked past the crime scene circles and explored the ground for some distance beyond. We watched him as he stopped, nudged something in the grass with his foot.

"You find something?" the girl called to him.

"Somebody had a horse out here not long ago," he said, turning and coming back to join his friends. "Maybe he was shot from horseback."

"Wow, a horse on a ranch, imagine that," the second boy said. "You find hoofprints, Sherlock?"

"Droppings. Fresh enough to still flatten with your foot."

"Wipe your feet before you get back in my pickup."

The girl looked at her watch. "Come on, let's go. I don't mind skipping class, but I've got to be home on time or my mom will yell at me."

They left. As the sound of the pickup retreated, the silence returned. Nothing but the graded road marked humanity's presence. The Indians said the Great Spirit, after making the earth, dumped the leftover rock into the Trans-Pecos. Looking at the gravelly soil, the piled-up mountains, flat-topped, domed, razor-backed, all awe-inspiring, I could believe it. Ranching did not come to the Trans-Pecos until after the Indian Wars. From then until the forties, only a moment in geologic time, those mountains had witnessed great change. Surveying parties marked off sections; cattle, sheep, and horses brought by trail, and later rail, grew sleek on the rich grasses; newcomers dug wells and installed windmills, established towns, and ended the open range. Then came the overgrazing, worsened by the ten years of drought in the fifties that all but wiped out the grasslands. Yet here I stood between vaulted sky and open plain, below mountains that were all but timeless. I shook myself back to the present and the murder that had been the end of one man's time.

I didn't know what I'd expected to see, but I lived close enough to Mexico to feel the pull of the site of a death. I liked the Mexican custom of marking the spot where a loved one died in an accident. Roadside *descansos*—memorial tokens—of crosses or flowers, marked the back roads and highways of Mexico and on our side of the river for as long as road crews left them. Would Ella bring flowers here? Who else would mourn for Julian Row?

I turned the pickup toward home. As I passed the cutoff to the sisters' ranch, the sheriff's Crown Victoria pulled out heading in the opposite direction. I could see the taillights pop on and off, and I guessed that he watched me in his rearview mirror.

Because of my detour, Clay had reached home before me. He stood at the refrigerator removing roast beef and salad makings.

"Have you fed Phobe?"

"Of course."

After we ate, we compared notes on what we had learned about Row's murder. "I just finished calling you about the starter when Tate arrived with the news," Clay said. "I thought it must have been an accident, but I guess not, if it was a close shot."

"That's what Tate told the Spiveys. And in daylight. I know that road is used only by a handful of ranchers, but still. . . . Who takes a chance like that?"

"Whoever killed Row did."

"There's something else I'd better tell you," I said. "Leila admitted to me she put peyote in one of the drinks. It was meant for Row."

"Is she crazy? Where did she get it?"

"Among all the other things in the Spivey house is a collection of potted cacti. Probably some of them came from Mexico and one of them is peyote."

"I'll adjust her bill accordingly."

"That's just the beginning." I recounted the rest of my conversation with Leila, including what she asked me to do.

"If you warn Howie and he runs, he'll look guilty," Clay said. "That's assuming he isn't. Not to mention phrases that spring to mind like *aiding and abetting*. Leila must have lost her mind to suggest such a thing."

"Leila isn't assuming he's innocent. She made that plain, although she stopped short of actually saying so. She seemed more worried about Howie than about the shock Ella's had. Of course she has more sympathy for Howie. She thinks Ella has made a fool of herself and her sisters."

"That foolishness is history. The great myth maker has told his last tale."

"I just can't get over Leila. She told me—what were

her words?—'I don't lie well.' Maybe not, but it's not what people say, it's what they keep silent about that's revealing. I'm wondering, what else might she have tried in order to be rid of him."

TWELVE

I heard the sound of the motor and the scrunch of gravel as a vehicle pulled in, but I gave the trading post sign one last good rub with the soapy rag before climbing down from the ladder to wait on the customer. It was Saturday morning. For over an hour, atop the tall ladder, I had towered over the pilgrims while they prayed. I was removing the smoke stain graying the bright yellow and red of the sign Cadillac Charlie had painted for me the previous Christmas.

The pilgrims and I had agreed on a routine. They were free to pray and light candles to *Nuestra Señora* from sunup to sundown. No candles burning during the night. No blocking the lot in front of the trading post. Best of all, soon they could buy all the candles they wanted from me. Clay was bringing me back a supply from Presidio. He'd asked Ruben Reyes to take him into town so he could drive the vetmobile home.

As I folded the ladder back out of the way, a tentative voice said, "*Con permiso*, señora."

I turned my head and looked into the face of Barrilito. I looked closer, saw this man was younger, and slipped into Spanish. "You must be a relative of"—I almost said Barrilito before catching myself and recalling what the sheriff had said was the photographer's real name—"Vicente Soto."

Looking relieved, he explained that he spoke no English and was grateful for my Spanish, and, yes, he was Vicente Soto's eldest son, Roberto, and he had come with his half brothers to see the place where his father died. A Ojinaga cab driver had given him directions.

I expressed my sorrow at his father's death and wiped my damp hands against my jeans to dry them. I felt the thick callouses on his palms as we shook hands solemnly and I said I'd show him where his father fell.

"My half brothers wait in the pickup," he said, motioning to them to join us. There were four others, each so like his father they might have been cloned.

Roberto explained that they had walked from the far side of Ojinaga, across the bridge, and into Presidio, where the authorities had released their father's vehicle to them. The brothers had brought with them a hand-cast concrete cross on a pedestal base. One of the brothers lifted it from the bed of the pickup and carried it to the spot I showed them.

"Just there," I said. He placed the cross upright on its base. Another brother set a blue glass vase at the foot of the cross, and a third carefully put plastic flowers in the vase. The *descanso* in place, I moved away and went to the porch to give them some privacy. It was a sad sight, the five stocky men, dark heads bowed, work-roughened hands clasped, standing around the cross beside the road against the desolate backdrop of scorched earth stretching to the river and far beyond. After the prayer, they went together and lit a candle for *Nuestra Señora*.

A few minutes later, they gathered in a conversation near the truck, going through their pockets and putting their cash together. I realized they might not have enough gasoline to get home and maybe not enough money to buy what they needed. The funeral expense had to be met, too, and that would be enough of a hardship. I slipped inside, went to the register, and counted out fifty dollars.

The bell jangled as Roberto came in, a strained look on his tired face. Before he could hold out the thin fold of worn bills he held in his hand, I said, "I'm glad you came in. I was going to give you this." I handed him the cash.

"What is this?" he asked.

"Money people owed your father for photographs he took of them. They paid me after his death."

"Our father never went anywhere without his camera, I know. *Gracias*. This will be a great help. We will get gas while we are here. We will fill up the tank."

While one of his half brothers ran the pump, Roberto asked me to point out on the wall map where Marfa was. I showed him and then, knowing why he asked, I found a map of Marfa and marked the location of the funeral home. After the autopsy, his father's body would be released to the funeral home, the only one in Presidio County. Most of the time, when a Mexican national died in Presidio County, family members would drive across, pick up the casket, load it into the pickup, and drive back home.

As they prepared to leave, Roberto said, "We have yet to receive our father's body, but we will send word of the funeral, should you wish to attend."

They drove away, two of the men riding in the pickup's cab, the others huddled in the back end.

I settled behind the counter, taking out the cash box to replenish the register. I was counting out bills when the bell sounded again and Claudia Reyes come in. Claudia walks with her head and shoulders tilted forward as if she's always in a hurry. Everything about the cook and owner of La Casa Azul restaurant is rounded, face, features, even her pink-framed glasses. Of average height, her thick body makes her appear shorter. Her rich brown hair, as always, was neatly permed and set in a short style framing her face and she wore one of the bright-colored dresses she favored.

"What can I do for you, Claudia? I have fresh chile pepper in from New Mexico." Claudia buys most of her restaurant supplies through the trading post, except for meat. For that, her husband Ruben buys a goat or cow from one of the local ranches and butchers it himself.

"I'll take the chile pepper, of course. I came to ask if I could borrow your set of butcher knives. Ruben and I are planning a barbecue for the marines as a thank-you for saving our homes from the fire. Ruben has asked Juan and Lupe from the Fall-Back Ranch to help him with the butchering and he needs another set of knives."

Free-range hen may be all the rage at trendy restaurants, but free-range beef tastes nothing like the feed-lot, grain-fed meat that one buys in the supermarket. I'd never developed a taste for the strong, rather gamey flavor. Ruben Reyes was the only person I knew who could prepare it so that it was tender and tasty. The spices he used helped, that and slow cooking in a pit.

"What a great idea. I'll be glad to do anything to help. We certainly owe the soldiers. Count on me for soft drinks, paper napkins, and plates."

"No, no, Texana. We will buy them from you. You do too much as it is."

"Help yourself to the knives. You know where they are." When she returned from the kitchen with the knives in their case, I filled her large order from her list and together we carried the bags to her van.

I spent the next hour and fifteen minutes waiting on other customers, one a rancher who, complaining that his fence line along the river was cut, rolled up, and carried off as fast as he could build it, bought a roll of barbed wire and three pairs of work gloves.

When Sheriff Tate showed up unexpectedly, I was loading range cubes into the back of Gwen Masters's pickup. The lack of rain meant we were headed into winter short of grass. Gwen was feeding two and a half pounds a day per animal to keep her cattle healthy through the dry weather and put some weight on them for the cold winter ahead. Nights chill down to the low teens in the Marfa highlands.

"What's he in such an all-fired hurry for?" Gwen said as the sheriff passed by without so much as a nod and went inside.

I could only shrug. Gwen went on her way and I went inside to see what the sheriff wanted.

It didn't take long to find out. The sheriff stood just inside the door, waiting for me.

"I see the Soto family has put up a memorial. I'd like to know what you talked about."

I told him about the Soto brothers' visit. He nodded and said, "I see.

"And this man's family didn't have a clue why he was killed?"

"I didn't ask."

"Did they ask anything about how he died? Why here? How you came to find him?"

"No."

"Don't you find that odd?"

"No. I assume they know about his finger being cut off. If they know that, they know why he was murdered. Under those circumstances I hardly think they'd be asking questions."

He gave a grunt of dissatisfaction. "This Soto clan you say you know nothing about, they come here, ask no questions, put up that cross out there, say a prayer, and go home. I never knew a Mexican not to have vengeance in his heart when family is killed. Maybe that cross was an excuse for them to pay you a visit, take up where their daddy left off in the drug smuggling. Too many coincidences around here. Your husband gets high on something in Marfa. I know. He claims it was food poisoning. I asked around. He ate from a vendor's booth, same as everybody. Nobody else in the whole town got sick from bad food. A man is murdered right here. It's a drug killing. All these marines hanging around. Mexicans from the other side camping out, supposedly to pray to that image out there. Good cover for anything you wanted to move across the river. Money flows one way, drugs another."

I held up a hand, trying to interrupt the flow, but the sheriff ignored me to swing a bony arm toward the Rio Grande. "It's how far from this building to the nearest river crossing that you can drive?"

"With the river this low, you can cross just about anywhere right now."

Tate said, "Convenient. It would be a lot better for you to come clean about what's going on here, than for me to dig it out on my own. Funny thing, the sheriffing around here was real peaceful until the past few months. Now I've got two murders, and the only common denominator is the Joneses. The vet is at the Spiveys every other day, it seems like. You're there when I come to tell the old ladies about Row's murder."

In the face of his vehemence, I'd given up any attempt at arguing.

"A lot of your customers come from the other side, don't they?" His question in the midst of the diatribe caught me by surprise, and all I could manage was a mumbled, "Yes."

"More then half?"

"About half."

"I guess they wouldn't feel too comfortable if the Border Patrol parked along the road right out front. Think about it."

"Sheriff, I don't—"

"Then there are the marines. New faces, new customers. Maybe some with a taste for drugs. Buy cheap this close to the source and take it home. Strikes me as a real business opportunity for a place like this, with no drive-by traffic, not much business in the normal way of things. Maybe it was you this photographer was pointing the finger at."

"Sheriff, murder isn't good for business. Just the opposite. The only business opportunity I've taken advantage of is the Madonna on the wall of this trading post, and even a miraculous image doesn't seem to protect me from your suspicions."

"That image is as phony as your candor," he said, giving me a cold smile.

143

THIRTEEN

Sunday afternoon is the one day a week we allow ourselves the luxury of an afternoon nap. I was sleeping so soundly the telephone barely roused me. Not until Clay shook my shoulder and said, "It's Leila, for you," did I wake fully.

"What hellish thing has happened now," I said, gently dislodging Phobe's head from where it rested heavily on my thigh. I heard the bobcat's displeased *merump*, as I went into the kitchen and picked up the receiver from the counter and answered rather curtly.

"You didn't warn Howie, did you? He was arrested this morning for Row's murder. I want to visit Cosmé. I prefer not to go alone and I don't want any of my sisters to go with me. Will you?"

"Cosmé is probably in Marfa with Howie, arranging bail or talking to a lawyer or something."

"I called. She's home. Please, Texana."

Please. From Leila Spivey, who I'd never heard say please unless she was asking you to pass the salt. Half of me wanted nothing to do with it. The other half wanted to find out what was going on. I gave in to vulgar curiosity.

I looked at the clock. It was a few minutes after two. "I'll pick you up around four-thirty."

In the bedroom, Clay was half-asleep again. When I told him where I was going, he mumbled, "You should have told her no" without opening his eyes. By the time I hit the kitchen for my keys, he was snoring.

Leila was thoughtful. She had driven as far as the gate to meet me and we went from there.

Cosmé Vega had a degree in range science from Sul Ross in Alpine. For three years before she became Mrs. Howie Crosswell, she had been manager of a ranch on the Casa Piedra Road. She had kept her job after marriage, living in a house on the ranch, a flat-roofed adobe set down among grama grasses. Next to it a long metal barn held ranch and road maintenance equipment, tack, and several stalls for horses.

Cosmé had heard us coming and waited in the open doorway. Looking taller than her medium height, she wore a long-sleeved red work shirt and saddle-polished jeans tucked into dusty cowhide boots. She had tied back the tips of her long crimped hair so that its fullness made a dark and heavy halo around her face, but couldn't fall in her way as she did ranch chores. Her brown skin had the sheen of vigorous health. She had a wide forehead, delicate eyebrows, and coffee-colored eyes that were rather small and tilted slightly upward at the edges, a straight nose widening at the tip, and full lips.

She stepped aside to let us enter. The front room must have taken up most of the house. The ceiling had hand-cut *vigas,* the walls were white, and the floor was a dark blue slate. A red leather couch dominated the room with comfortable armchairs and a few bright rugs as accessories. The walls had been decorated with antique branding irons, spurs, and other ranch para-phernalia. Nowhere did I see a single painting. Maybe Howie didn't want his art displayed in his home.

Leila lowered herself into an armchair. Cosmé sat on the couch, her legs stretched out and crossed at the ankles, her eyes judging us and, by her expression of distaste, finding us lacking. Her alert stillness seemed unnatural. And why not. Her husband had been ar-rested for murder. I sat in the other armchair and waited for one of them to say something.

Leila broke the silence. "I want to help Howie, Mrs. Crosswell. I like the boy and—"

"He is not a boy. He is a man." Cosmé's voice was low and soft, yet filled with authority. "Why do you want to help him? What have you to do with it?" Her last words were spoken not as a question, but as a challenge.

Leila slumped slightly in the chair. "Let me start

over. I want to help Howie because I know and like him. As you know, he used to work for us. If you and Howie will allow me, I'd like to help with some money toward his defense."

Cosmé nodded once, as if in acknowledgment of Leila's unspoken apology. "That would be acceptable. Provided, of course, that Howie agrees."

"Do you think he might not," I said, careful to keep my voice neutral.

Cosmé looked directly at me. "I know why she's here. Why are you? Do you want to contribute to the defense fund, too?"

"She drove me," Leila said.

That seemed to satisfy Cosmé. "Who knows what Howie will do or say? He has funny ideas sometimes about how things should be. I told him to call a lawyer this morning and he told me to mind my own business. He was drinking last night. As usual. He was still sleeping it off in his studio when the sheriff showed up with his deputy asking about where he was when this man Row was shot. I told them they'd have to ask Howie. They wouldn't let me go and wake him, but I followed them out to the studio. They shook him awake, he sat up and asked who he'd killed. The sheriff didn't laugh."

"Have you a lawyer in mind, Mrs. Crosswell?" Leila asked.

"Only a court-appointed one, until you showed up. Howie doesn't make any money because most of his paintings are hanging on the wall of his studio."

"I thought Howie's work was popular and selling well," I said, voicing my surprise.

Cosmé gave me a scornful look. "There isn't anything wrong with his work. He's had lots of requests from galleries that want to show his work. These paintings—come to the studio and see for yourself." She stood in one smooth, languid movement. I helped Leila get up and we followed Cosmé through a small kitchen and out the back door to what looked like an oversize wooden shed until we got inside. The light from a north-facing, plate glass window illuminated three walls of paintings done in vibrant tones. They varied in subject: a woman sitting outdoors beneath a canopy of trees, her feet dangling in the clear waters of a creek, a little boy and girl running across a field toward a house; a lovely golden-haired woman gathering roses. They went on and on, rows and rows, from floor to ceiling.

"You see," Cosmé said.

"He used the same models over and over," I said.

"She was his first wife. Those were their kids. That's all he does. Drink and paint them over and over. With the other paintings, his landscapes, he made little more than an *albañil*. Just a common laborer, that's all he was with his precious artwork. I said to him, if you want to paint your first wife, then at least sell the paintings. Make some money. I told him, better to be a well-known drunk than an anonymous alcoholic. How can you be well known if you don't sell paintings. But no, he wouldn't part with them."

"Did the sheriff see these?" I asked.

"Of course," Cosmé said. "He went through the house and the studio. This is where he found the gun."

Leila looked shocked. "What gun?"

Cosmé said merely, "The one that killed that man, I suppose."

Leila opened her pocketbook, took out a white business card, and handed it to Cosmé. "That's the name of a lawyer that's done business for my family for a long time. I don't know that he takes criminal cases, but he can get you someone who does."

"I'll give this to Howie." Cosmé slipped the card into her breast pocket, then went to the door and held it open for us, making it clear the visit was over. I followed Leila out and we walked around the house to the pickup.

Leila buckled up and said so softly she might have been speaking to herself, "Why did he leave the gun in his studio?"

"If it is the murder weapon," I said, negotiating around an eroded part of the ranch road, "and we don't know that yet, and neither does the sheriff until it's tested—then admittedly, it was a stupid thing to do. But Howie had no reason to think he'd be suspected. Could he? Leila, you didn't tell him about that detective agency report, did you?"

"Of course not." She said it so firmly, I believed her and she looked so exhausted, I made no more comments, asked no more questions.

A few miles down the road, Leila said, "It didn't go well with Cosmé, did it?"

"She's had a very bad morning. I can understand why she might be hesitant to commit to anything right now. Especially before talking to Howie. My guess is you'll hear from her. What's she got to lose?"

We reached the pavement. I waited ten minutes before dropping Leila a hint that I was curious about Howie's wife by saying, "I met Howie just the one time, at his first exhibit. That must have been before he got married. I never met Cosmé until today."

"And I didn't introduce you. I'm sorry," Leila said. "I always thought she had set her cap for the lawyer that owns the ranch, but it hadn't happened in the first three years she had worked for him, so when Howie came along . . . Cosmé grew up on the Howell Ranch. Her mother cooked for the cowhands. The father was a part-time ranch hand and a full-time drunk. It got so bad he finally couldn't get any work. That child worked hard to get out from under that."

"Howie's drinking must have hit her especially hard, then," I said.

"She seemed purely crazy about him when they married. I think she thought him being an artist was romantic. She saw something she thought she wanted and maybe found out too late she didn't."

When we finally got to the ranch gate and Leila's vehicle, it was well after dark and she looked so tired I suggested she let me drive her to the house. She agreed, saying, "I'll send Pitt down for the truck in the morning."

I pulled up by the front door. Leila seemed to almost fall from the seat and stood holding the door to steady herself. Hattie opened the door, took one look at Leila, and said, "You silly old woman. You've worn yourself out. Let me help you. Come on in, Texana, and have some coffee. It's ready and waiting."

I wanted to go home, but Leila was leaning so heavily on Hattie, I took her other arm to help them inside. The sisters were sitting in front of a television badly in need of a color adjustment, but as soon as they saw me, Mattie, using both hands to work the remote, cut it off. Two other sisters, remotes in hand, were slower on the draw. After that, I felt I had to accept the offer of coffee. It came on a tray set with porcelain cups and saucers decorated with the ranch brand. "Mother and Daddy's fiftieth anniversary present," Hattie explained. As Clara served us, I noticed one of the sisters was missing.

"I hope Ella's not ill," I said, thinking of her collapsed face the day of Row's murder.

"She's fine. She's all settled in."

"She's in bed?"

"She's in Florida," Clara said. "Some old friends are going to take her on a cruise. Leila thought it best . . ."

". . . to get her mind off Mr. Row's tragic death," Hattie said.

"Well," I said. "She did say she'd always wanted to travel."

I left the ranch on a caffeine high from which I hadn't come down when I arrived home, hungry and irritable. The sight of the pristine 1955 white Cadillac parked in front of the trading post cheered me considerably.

In the living area, I found Clay and the owner of the car, our old friend Cadillac Charlie, talking and laughing and drinking whiskey.

Clay said, "I hope you're hungry, hon, because Charlie cooked his quick and easy chili."

My mouth watered at the thought. Charlie's recipe takes thirty minutes and is the best chili I've ever eaten.

"Let me take my shoes off and have a whiskey, maybe two, and I'll be ready."

"We've got Lucy's homemade tortillas to eat with it," Clay said. "She brought them while you were gone."

"And I brought a brick of Monterey Jack cheese," Charlie added.

"Good whiskey, good food, and a good friend. I'm in heaven," I told him, raising my glass in a toast.

While I enjoyed a second whiskey and toasted my slippered feet in front of the fire, Clay ladled the chili into bowls and warmed the tortillas.

I was coffeed-out, but after we ate I made a pot for Clay and Charlie and we sat around the fireplace and caught up on the news. Charlie seems to know everyone in our part of *la frontera*. He's a modern gypsy. Tucked neatly into the trunk of his Cadillac is everything he needs: clothes, coffeepot, frying pan, Dutch oven, bedroll, and Coleman lamp. He travels our sixty miles of the border, keeping to no time schedule but his own, doing odd jobs and manual labor to pay his way. He works for me about twice a year in return for gas and groceries. Though I never know when he will show up or how long he will stay, Charlie is one of those people you're always glad to see. Soft-spoken and genial, he seldom talks about himself, but takes a great interest in the lives of others and because he listens, people talk to him, telling him things they'd hesitate to discuss with anyone else. Charlie is a person you can relax with.

He told us he'd been in Mexico helping a friend with a one-man adobe brick works. We caught him up on the road building, the fire, and finally the murder of the street photographer. Not surprisingly, Charlie had known him.

"Poor Barrilito," Charlie said. "I always thought he'd die from one wife too many. He always kept a *casita* of his own to get away from his responsibilities. Only he couldn't stop marrying and when he got himself a new wife, he'd have to move her into his *casita*, turning it into a *casa chica*. Then, he'd have to find a new place for himself."

Finally, we got around to telling Charlie about the murder of Julian Row. Though Charlie knew of the Spivey family, he'd never worked for them and hadn't heard a whisper about Row. Charlie's deep knowledge of local life and residents stops short of Marfa. He's all *fronterizo*.

153

"That reminds me," Clay said, "what did Leila want? If you told me before you left, I was too sleepy to take it in."

I got as far as, "When she found out Howie Crosswell had been arrested for Row's murder—"

Charlie sat up so fast I heard his spine pop. "Howie? Why is he supposed to have killed this guy Row?"

Clay quietly asked a question of his own. "You know Crosswell, Charlie?"

"He's a veteran, like me. Different war. The Gulf War wasn't 'Nam. But I understand why he came to the Trans-Pecos. War saturates you with people as well as blood. To survive afterward, you have to find someplace with space. I think each person has a built-in stress quota. When that's used up, you have to be careful of yourself. Like your dad, Texana. That's what Howie came here for. The grant to paint, that was part of it, but whether he realizes it or not, the place was what he'd been looking for. Vets are never the same coming out of a war as they were going in. You carry a gut-deep grief around with you. It doesn't matter if you slashed away one man's life with a bayonet or left a whole unit of the enemy floundering in a fire bomb. Once you've killed, once you've gone past hope into that moment when all that holds you together is the power you have to kill. Once you've watched men who are your friends die like cattle, you've crossed a line. It's not a line in the sand. The wind can't wipe it away."

The ticking of the clock resounded in the moment

of silence that followed Charlie's words. I had known he'd been a helicopter pilot in Vietnam, but never before, not by so much as a word, had he spoken of the war nor about its effect on him.

Charlie reacted first, blinking rapidly like a sleeper waking into the too-bright light of day. "Sorry," he said. He got up from the chair. "I think I'll get out my bedroll and pack it in for tonight. Maybe tomorrow I'll drive up to Marfa and see if Howie needs anything."

Before Clay or I recovered, Charlie was gone, moving with a grace and dexterity surprising in so heavy a man.

"God help him," I said. Most of my prayers are fitful things, but this one was heartfelt. Clay slipped his arm around my shoulders.

"Howie certainly has supporters," he said. "First Leila Spivey, now Charlie."

"I wonder."

"Wonder what?"

"Leila feels guilty about that report. Charlie has personal emotions about his experience in Vietnam and projects that onto Howie. Their interest in the man seems entirely personal. I wonder how well either of them really knows him."

FOURTEEN

How easily I let myself be lulled into thinking I had nothing to worry about. The Lincoln Flat murder, as people referred to the shooting of Julian Row, involved people of standing in the community, chiefly the Spivey family, but also the artist under arrest. The sheriff would be too busy, I thought, to trouble himself further over my connection to Barrilito. So much for assumptions.

"That Sheriff Tate is asking questions about you," Claudia said. She had come especially to warn me. "He went from house to house. He wanted to know about *forajeros* and *extranjeros* that come to the trading post."

Foreigners and strangers. Tate might not know *la*

frontera culture well enough to understand the law of silence that governs much of the border, but Deputy Rano Johnson knew it well. In isolated communities like ours we handled problems from within. Border-landers had minds of their own about the laws of the heartland from which we were separated by state of mind and circumstance as much as immense distances. For generations our stretch of the border had been ig-nored by the politicians and on the odd occasion that attention was paid, it was likely to be in the mistaken application of laws designed to please the population centers while making it harder for us to conduct the normal cross-border social, business, and cultural life that both unite and divide us. Some laws are incom-patible with the realities of border life, and *fronterizos* are adroit at violating the letter of the law in order to make workable a life on a frontier that is neither wholly American nor wholly Mexican in spirit and un-derstanding.

I smiled at the thought of Tate questioning what I thought of as my extended family. "What did you say?"

"The marines are the only strangers I've seen, I told him." She took something out of her pocket and pressed it into my hand. "This is for you, for protec-tion from that Tate's bad thoughts and from the peo-ple who killed the photographer. You take care, Texana. You have been blessed with the image of *Nuestra Señora de la Factoría,* and the devil will be jealous and set evil in your path."

Hearing that, I felt a little less complaisant. I waved as she drove away, then looked at the religious medal. It had the image of Saint Michael the Archangel, carrying a sword. An armed warrior. I slipped the chain over my head and around my neck. Howie had Leila and Charlie as his champions. I had Claudia and Saint Michael.

The telephone was ringing as I stepped back inside. Whoever it was remained persistent as I made my way to the back to answer on the ninth ring.

Assuming my identity from my "hello," the caller moved directly to his point. "Have you received the package I shipped to Fran at your address? I called her and she said she hadn't gotten it."

"Jake? The package! It came. I'd forgotten all about it. I'll call Fran."

"My fault. I forgot she was staying at the Paisano. If you could find the time to get it to her, I'd appreciate it. You'll be doing me a great favor."

I told him I would do my best. We asked each other the usual family-type questions, being more polite than interested. After we disconnected, I went to the front and fumbled beneath the counter where I put UPS packages shipped to the trading post in other people's names, usually ranchers along the back reaches above the river or Mexicans from the other side of the river, who come in when the spirit moves them. I found the package and pulled it out. What was in it that was so important? I was in no mood to close the trading post and drive all the way to Marfa, not with the pilgrims outside. I'd been selling them enough food and drink to ensure a profit, hooray, for the month. Claudia was right. *Nuestra Señora* had blessed me.

When Clay is home he sometimes minds the trading post for me, but he'd been called out, so the package would have to wait. There was a limit to how often I could afford to close and I'd reached it.

Cadillac Charlie came toward me in his smooth glide, his thin brown hair neat and cut short, his soft blue eyes reflecting the smile he gave me. He'd been working on some changes to the clinic that Clay hadn't had time to make.

"That's all done. I framed in the new wall for the extra cages like Clay wanted. All he has to do is nail up the paneling. I thought I'd run into Presidio, get the paneling supplies, and finish the whole job for him, if that's okay."

I asked him for a favor instead and he agreed, saying, "That way, I can do what I said last night, stop and see how Howie is holding up. I'll still have time to do the paneling, if you know what kind Clay wants."

"Clay wants the least expensive, as long as it's sturdy and washable. Use your own judgment and charge it to our account." I gave him the package.

After he left, I called the Paisano. Fran was in. I told her the package was on its way and she laughed. "Jake is anxious because there's money involved. The package is a book Picasso's buying from him, something about the Civil War by a man named Heartsill. Jake got it from a client along with a lot of other books in lieu of a fee. It's been valued between eight and ten thousand dollars. Picasso is a Civil War buff. Guess what? We're going to be partners in an art gallery. Picasso already owns an old commercial building that will be perfect. All we have to do is repaint, get in a few quality furnishings, and decide on artists for the opening."

I wished her luck with the business venture and we hung up just as Clay came bustling in from the back, his arms loaded down with sacks that he put down on the counter.

"What's all that?" I asked.

"Used clothes from the rancher whose bull calf I doctored. She thought you could sell them."

"Leave them on the sale table. How's the patient?"

"Okay, or he will be. A castrating accident. The rancher used a Burdizzo and caught the wrong body part. Now the calf's a she, so to speak."

I reported to him about Charlie, told him what Fran had said, and last about Tate questioning our neighbors.

"That's not anything to worry about," Clay said. "There's no meat on that bone for him to chew."

The remainder of the afternoon was quiet, no customers for me, no clients calling for Clay. Even the pilgrims had thinned, many going home early. Charlie returned home at three. He and Clay went to work installing the paneling.

Shortly before five, Roberto Soto telephoned from

Ojinaga to say the funeral of his father would be held on Thursday at one P.M. at the Gonzales *Funeraria* of Ojinaga. I felt obligated to attend. The man had died in my front yard.

I locked up at six and Clay and Charlie came in shortly after, ready for dinner.

"This business with Howie looks bad," Charlie said, stroking Phobe, who had made herself at home in his lap while we ate. "I've offered to help him make bail. If he can get it. This close to Mexico, the district attorney will probably say Howie is a flight risk."

"The court will set a high bail, if any," Clay said.

Charlie nodded. "Howie isn't helping. I ran into Cosmé and she said he won't cooperate with the lawyer she hired."

"Has he denied the murder?" I asked.

"Yes. And that's all he's saying. Cosmé can't give him an alibi. The morning this Row fellow got shot, she was in the barn shoeing horses. She supposed Howie was in his studio painting like he did most days, but really she doesn't know where he was. She mentioned that this Miss Spivey you told me about was helping out with the lawyer fees. Cosmé thinks the lady feels guilty because it was information from her that got Howie arrested. I'm not sure what she meant."

I assumed Rano Johnson had told the sheriff about his call for Leila to the detective agency, and that the sheriff either had pressured Leila for the report or called the agency. I told Charlie about Leila Spivey having Row investigated, including the dead man's responsibility for the deaths of Howie's first wife and their two kids. "Did Cosmé tell you the sheriff found a gun in Howie's studio and took it away? She assumes it's the murder weapon."

"She didn't say anything to me about that," Charlie said. "I knew since the sheriff had already arrested Howie, he must be real confident in his ability to make a case. Now I see why. Tate must have marked 'rush' on the ballistics tag. The grand jury's already sitting. They can indict Howie in a day."

After dinner, Charlie went to the clinic to shower, then spread his bedroll in the front room and turned in. I closed the door to our quarters and Clay and I sat reading on the couch. At nine, Clay suggested a nightcap, and I joined him.

"Clay," I said tentatively, "maybe you should tell the sheriff about someone putting peyote in your drink."

Clay dropped another ice cube into my glass. "Tate doesn't listen. He jumps to conclusions. Besides that, the Spiveys are my clients, at least until the herd tests clean. No point in antagonizing them to no purpose. I sure don't think it'll budge Tate from his attitude. And if I make unprovable accusations toward the people as well thought of as the Spivey sisters, it could hurt my business."

I started to argue, when an unexpected sound came from the back door. It was Pete Rosales calling our names. I unlocked the door and welcomed him in.

"Great timing, Pete, we're having a whiskey. Join us?" Clay held out his untouched glass to Pete.

Pete sat down, smiling and at ease as he always is, and Clay fixed himself another drink, asking, "How'd you find things at home? Okay I hope."

"Man, we're fine. That's what I came to tell you guys. No damage except smoke. Those goats had everything so eaten down there was nothing to burn. The fire just went around us in a great big circle. Only thing we lost was the grandkids' plastic toys. What's been going on with you two? I hear things. Something about trouble."

Clay explained, including the sheriff's suspicions about Barrilito and drugs.

Pete shook his head in disbelief. "If this Barrilito was going to point the finger at somebody, he was crazy. Those drug lords, even the drug commoners— how you like my joke—are going to kill. Doesn't matter before or after you talk, you're dead. Even the people who want to keep their hands clean are too afraid to say no if they get pressured to move *la droga*."

I thought about my childhood, growing up in the trading post with my parents, playing with kids from both sides of the river, thinking the whole world spoke our mix of English and Spanish. In those early days I had thought our lives idyllic because they were.

I asked Pete if he wanted to get anything for Zeferina, but he said she was still using what we'd sent home with them. "She wouldn't let me rest until I came to tell you guys we was okay and all, and I been busy all day, so now I'm here."

We talked, as Pete and I mostly did when we got together, of old times and growing up in Polvo. Pete could tell a good story and Clay liked to listen to him. It was after midnight when he left.

The night was quiet, and I slept well. Judging by the rhythmic sound of Clay's snoring, so did he. I woke to the droning of a low-flying plane, probably a Border Patrol Cessna keeping an eye out for illegals and spying on the trading post for the sheriff. That man was making me paranoid.

Wednesday was business as usual for both of us. Clay made a few calls, and I waited on a few customers. Tomorrow Charlie would man the register, and we would go to Barrilito's funeral in Ojinaga.

FIFTEEN

We had arrived before the Soto relatives so we parked and waited on the dirt street in front of Gonzales *Funeraria,* a nondescript building in the middle of a run-down block of peeling stucco houses and storefronts with common walls that edged the street and faded one into another.

The cement block funeral home's double doors looked as if they had come from a church. The Sotos arrived in two vehicles, the half brothers in the same pickup they had driven to the trading post, the women and children crammed together in a Chrysler New Yorker built before automobile downsizing. It took the tightly squeezed second group some minutes to disembark from their transport. They gathered on the narrow sidewalk.

"You could house a family in that car," Clay said.

"With all the wives Barrilito had to support, maybe he did," I said. "Shall we get out?"

We joined the Sotos. As Roberto took the arm of a gray-haired woman with rounded shoulders to lead the family inside, a truck bumped down the potholed street and turned into the drive of the funeral home. It was an old bread truck, the logo painted over in white but bleeding through. The driver stopped and let out a passenger who walked around the truck and toward the Sotos. The man wore a khaki uniform with no badge, the symbol of his authority a chrome-plated .45 automatic in a holster attached to his tooled-leather belt. Beside me I sensed Clay tense, as I did, in anticipation of trouble. In Mexico, an official presence is not comforting.

The women, herding the children before them, shuffled past the men to the security of the inside. I held back to listen to what happened as Barrilito's sons talked with the policeman.

He spoke pleasantly of "tragic loss" and "deepest sympathies" before delivering the punch line. "I came for the body," he said. "It is in our custody."

"Why?" one of the half brothers asked.

"Your father died in violence. There must be an official examination of the body."

For a moment no one spoke. The half brothers knew their father's body would have arrived from the United

States already embalmed. They knew also it would do no good to dispute the point.

Clay tugged at my arm, indicating we should go inside, but I stayed put and continued eavesdropping. One of the half brothers asked, "How much will it take to get the paperwork done without delaying the funeral of our father?"

"In dollars? I prefer dollars. Five hundred."

Roberto looked at his half brothers, apparently seeing agreement in their eyes, because he took out his billfold and slowly counted five bills into the upturned palm of the policeman.

I turned away, grabbed Clay's arm, and hurried him into the tiny anteroom of the funeral home. We seemed to startle the funeral director, a sloop-shouldered fellow with oiled hair and a black coat frayed with age. He directed us by pointing a finger toward Chapel B. The small room had dingy walls, worn carpet, and a plywood lectern, all illuminated by two lightbulbs dangling from the ceiling. A tape recording of guitars and trumpets blared out hymns. A horseshoe-shaped floral tribute stood out against the other bouquets of red and white flowers arranged on either side of a white-draped table intended for the casket. A photograph of Barrilito stood on an easel.

As Clay and I took our seats at the back, the half brothers entered, joining their families. The women had arranged themselves about the eight rows of the pews. After everyone else was seated, a young woman, heavily pregnant, her long hair hanging down her back, arrived unaccompanied and seated herself beside me. Her eyes were red from crying and she held a wadded handkerchief in her hand. One of the seated women stood up and approached her, hissed *puta*, and returned to her pew.

Five minutes went by. From a side door, six dark, stocky Indian men carried in the casket and placed it on the table. One of the Indians tugged a rag from his pocket and gave the brass handles a wipe while another raised the lid, and then they withdrew.

In the midst of the murmuring of the children, the shushings from their mothers, and the creaking of the pews, a man in a shiny suit and swept-back hair came in and took his place behind the lectern. The loud music ceased. He raised his hands and after a mention of Barrilito, spent the next twenty minutes sweatily haranguing us. When he finished, Roberto stepped forward and respectfully placed a white envelope in his hand. The preacher slipped it into an inside pocket and placed a hand on Roberto's shoulder before disappearing through the door by which he had entered. Who among the sons had hired the Pentecostal evangelist? Most of the women clutched rosaries in their hands and crossed themselves in silent prayer during the service.

Afterward, the half brothers stood on both sides of the coffin and the women moved forward to view the body. My own inclination toward burial is closed casket, but I dutifully moved forward behind the rest and paid my last respects to Barrilito. The funeral home in the United States had done its best, but without any idea of how the living man had looked, they had arranged the slack muscles of the dead face by guesswork. The body bore little resemblance to the man. Adding to the impression of a wax figure on display, the *funeraria* had followed the custom of Mexico, where embalming is seldom done, and fitted a sheet of glass over the corpse.

As the families embraced and consoled one another, the Indians appeared again, hoisted the casket shoulder high, and slow-marched it down the aisle and outside to the waiting hearse. A motorcycle cop in full uniform waited, ready to escort the vehicle. The Indians slid the casket into the back. The sons followed, carrying the flowers, and banked them around the casket. We waited respectfully as the families sorted themselves into their vehicles. A door slammed and from the house across the street a barefooted man carrying a trumpet in one hand hurried over. He stood in the middle of the road and played the long notes of something that sounded like music for the bullring. The motorcycle pulled out into the empty street. As the pickup carrying the half brothers drove past the trumpeter, a hand held out a peso note. The trumpeter snatched it, making a deep bow to the back of the last vehicle as it passed before turning and disappearing into his house. The short funeral procession went up the hill toward the cemetery.

"Clay," I said as we got into the pickup and buckled up, "a few days ago Barrilito's sons didn't have enough money among them to buy gas to get home. Today they paid off a cop in American dollars. And how did they afford a casket with brass handles, all those fresh flowers, and the motorcycle escort? I know Mexican families spend as lavishly as they can for a funeral, but poor families barely manage the cheapest casket. Barrilito worked the *zócalo* in Ojinaga with his camera. This wasn't the funeral of a street vendor. Where did the Sotos get the money?"

"I think we both have a good idea about that," Clay said. "I'm also thinking we may have made a big-time mistake showing up for this funeral. Let's get out of here."

"I want to talk to Charlie. He knew about Barrilito's wives. Maybe he knows more."

Clay negotiated Ojinaga's dusty gray streets carefully, slowing to a crawl and keeping our speed under the limit. Older American cars and trucks with Chihuahua plates made up much of the traffic, though Texas plates were common. Twice we saw Mercedes, both black with heavily tinted windows, and followed by Suburbans full of bodyguards, both concrete signs of drug culture wealth. During the eighties drug gangs had dominated the town, buying up businesses and donating money for fiestas and cockfights, while their teenage gangsters openly carried Uzis and AR-15s. Street gunfights were not uncommon. That stopped after one drug lord had bragged too freely to reporters from the United States at a time when city authorities were making a crackdown. The talkative and admired drug trafficker was gunned down in a shoot-out with federal police, yet his name lived on in the town's cantinas and in at least one *corrido* ballad. Beneath today's calmer outer surface, the gangs still ruled, despite or perhaps with the help of a heavy military presence in the town of thirty thousand people.

We crossed the International Bridge over the Rio Grande. The streets of Presidio were busy with traffic, many with orange *frontera* plates from Mexico, making the small town seem larger than it was. Clay turned west onto the empty river road.

Charlie sat on the porch enjoying the temperate fall afternoon and munching on a candy bar. "Two customers," he reported, closing his book. "One cash, one credit. Joe and Oscar came in right after you left."

Joe and Oscar were Border Patrol agents. Most of the agents who worked the river road came in from time to time to pick up local gossip. Their stopping wasn't odd. Charlie's making particular mention of it was.

"Anything unusual about their visit?" I asked him.

"They had loose eyes, looking around, noticing every little thing, like somebody looking for what others want hidden."

"Anything else?"

"They asked where you were. I told them and they left. Oscar was on the radio as they drove off."

Out here, local, state, and federal law enforcement agencies help each other out. It's a necessity caused by manpower shortages and distance. It seemed the sheriff had the Border Patrol keeping an eye on my business and my whereabouts.

"I'm going to fix us some iced tea," Clay said, going inside. I stayed on the porch with Charlie.

"How did the funeral go?" he asked.

"For the family of a street photographer, it must have cost plenty. Expensive casket, lots of flowers." I told Charlie about the other details. "Did you ever hear any rumors about Barrilito being mixed up with the drug trade?"

"That's not a thing people talk about until somebody gets caught or buried. I'll tell you, the men who keep *casas chicas* have to be able to afford it. Barrilito had a long string. He had to have money coming in from something on the side, but if he did, you'd never guess it from his house."

"You know where he lived?"

"Sure. I know most of the men and women who work the *zócalo* in OJ. Barrilito lived in a one-room adobe behind a *mecánico*."

Clay brought glasses of strong iced tea and plates of pimento cheese sandwiches. As I ate I tried to relax, but Charlie's words about the Border Patrol nosing around only added to my worries. Leila was right, innocence was not necessarily a strong enough defense. I reached up to my neck and fingered the Saint Michael medal Claudia had given me. I might need a miracle.

As the sun dropped low, so did the temperature. From somewhere along the river a breeze lifted the musky scent of javelina. We sat and watched the shadows envelope the mountains. A small nighthawk glided into the last light, crying its plaintive *poor will, poor will.* The volcanic cobbles cast dense little shadows and the burn scars of the mesquite and salt cedar trees vanished into the consuming dark. We live in the shadows of two majestic mountain ranges cast up sixty-five million years ago, the Sierra Madre Oriental and the Sierra Madre Occidental. The eastern mountains block winds from the Gulf of Mexico and the western range blocks the Pacific currents. Between them, the air is trapped and warmed, causing a dry season that extends from late October into early June. It would take next summer's seasonal rains to reconstitute the desert. When the Spanish arrived here, they found people living a pastoral life in the rich greenbelt of the river. Conquered by Spain, exterminated or sold as slaves, the names of those tribes, Jumanos, Conchos, Tobasos, Saliñeros, Chisos, Coahueleños, Cabazas, and Tepeguanes, have slipped from time and memory, as has the grand flow of the river they knew. The desert alone remained unconquered.

SIXTEEN

The pounding on the front doors came at one A.M. Clay threw back the covers, pulled on his pants, and grabbed a shirt and pistol, the latter tucked in the back waistband of his pants. I reached for my robe and slipped my feet into tennis shoes. In front, the porch light was on and Charlie was talking to someone standing just outside. As soon as he unlocked the doors, Irene Pick the schoolteacher came in carrying a towel-wrapped bundle with a furry golden tail hanging out.

"I heard Tyke screaming and I ran out and a coyote had him in its mouth, but it dropped him. He's bleeding."

"Let's get him to the surgery," Clay told her, leading the way toward the back.

I turned on the lights and opened the back door for Irene, who headed straight for the clinic. Clay got his keys from the peg by the door, jogged ahead of Irene, unlocked the office door, and reached in to cut on the lights. Clay followed Irene inside and closed the door. I checked on Phobe to be sure she was still sleeping on our bed. Raised with a puppy, she loves dogs, but she's unused to domestic cats. I closed the bedroom door so if she decided to roam, there would be no surprises.

"I'm going to fix some coffee," I told Charlie. He came with me and sat at the kitchen table. Accustomed to sleeping in his car or on a bedroll, Charlie wore his jeans, an outsize T-shirt, and thick white socks. I put the filter and coffee in the machine and took down the white cafe cups from their hooks under the plate rack. I thought some food might be needed so I thawed ten slices of bread in the microwave, spread them on a cookie sheet, sprinkled them with sugar-cinnamon mix, placed several dots of butter on each, and put them under the broiler.

Charlie had eaten three slices by the time Irene came in. "He's okay," she said, relief shining on her face. She shoved a hand through her thick gray hair. "Clay wanted to take some X rays. He said as soon as he checked the results, I could probably take Tyke home."

I poured her a cup of coffee.

We talked about how the "military highway" was coming. The marines were working far enough up river that I no longer heard the sound of the heavy equipment grinding away at leveling the rock and grading the roadway.

"Speaking of the marines," I said, "I haven't seen them for a while."

Irene had her cup halfway to her lips. She put it down and a frown creased her forehead. "Texana, I thought you'd know. The trading post has been placed off-limits to them."

"What? Why?" Then I answered my own question. "The shooting. I guess the sheriff must have talked to the officer in charge."

"Actually," Irene said hesitantly, "I heard he and a deputy questioned some of the marines."

"I should have realized he would do that."

Tactfully, Irene changed the subject to her granddaughter and my godchild, whose mother Elvia had started freshman courses at Sul Ross University in Alpine.

When Clay came in he was all smiles and carrying a sleek, yellow tabby. Irene raised her hands and took Tyke into her lap. Clay went to the cupboard, got out a small jar that he opened, spooning its contents into a saucer. He brought it over and held it briefly under the cat's nose, then set it on the floor. Tyke leaped down and licked eagerly from the saucer, waving his tail back and forth across the floor.

"What is that you gave him?" Irene said.

"Chicken-flavored baby food. Cats love it as a treat or when they're sick. It's almost predigested and the smell is strong so it stimulates their appetite."

"He's okay, then?"

"Full of fight. But I'd lock up that cat door at night from now on. Nine lives aren't nearly enough with all the predators we have around here."

Charlie walked Irene to her car and helped her settle the cat into his carrier. Clay went back to bed, I locked the rear door, and joined him.

It was Friday, another day in Presidio for Clay. He left after breakfast. Charlie did some more work on the addition to Clay's office and I waited on customers renting videos if they were staying home for the weekend, or buying gasoline if they were going into Presidio or over to Ojinaga to one of the restaurants.

Around ten, Pablo Pacheco's mother and aunt came in to shop. Pablo sat on the front steps, and Charlie joined him, taking a jar of liquid soap. The two sat shoulder to shoulder as Charlie showed Pablo how to dip the plastic ring into the jar and blow bubbles that floated away on the breeze, making miniature rainbows in the sunlight. Seeing Pablo reminded me that I hadn't yet returned the deputy's badge to Rano Johnson. I took the shiny badge out and put it on top of the register where I wouldn't forget it the next time I saw the deputy, which was likely to be any time, the way things were going. After the Pachecos left, I asked Charlie how he'd like lunch in Ojinaga, my treat.

He smiled. "You want to see where Barrilito lived."

"And go inside if we can do it without drawing attention to ourselves." After the funeral, I had asked

Charlie if he could tell me anything more about the man, but it seemed there wasn't much more than we'd already discussed. Barrilito had been one of a handful of street vendors of various sorts who worked the main square in Ojinaga and who Charlie knew to say hello to and pass the time of day with. Barrilito had bragged to Charlie about his many wives.

Two hours later we passed the *aduana*, customs, and entered Mexico. Ojinaga's street are narrow and filled with cars, vendors pushing carts, and pedestrians. People congregated in doorways, spilling over onto the cracked ribbon of sidewalk and into the street.

I parked on the street in front of a little restaurant I know on the Calle Juarez, its only sign a hand-printed placard in the window. Zoco, the owner, cook, and cashier, was wiping down the counter in the narrow little front room. The place smelled of hot lard and chile peppers. The only other person in the tiny restaurant was a tired-looking man eating at the end of the counter. He nodded to us, said *buenos tardes*, and went back to his food. We perched on rickety wooden stools. There was no menu at Zoco's. He prepared a specialty of the day, his choice determined by what he had bought at the market plus a strong measure of personal whim.

He greeted us warmly, announcing the day's special as *budín Azteca*, served us the Mexican beers we ordered, and vanished into the kitchen, returning in a few minutes with two steaming plates on which he'd spooned generous portions of the spicy casserole, a mix of tortillas, chiles, chicken, cheese, and sour cream. We ate in silence, enjoying the food.

Back in the pickup, I eased into the traffic and Charlie directed me as I drove. We left the main street, where new homes of brick hugged the curb, passed under a low bridge, and hit an unpaved street thick with dust that left a smothering cloud in our wake as we made our way slowly west. The adobes grew smaller and smaller as we neared the edge of town. Finally, Charlie pointed out a small auto repair shop where a shirtless man worked on an engine suspended from a rope looped over a tree limb and tied at the other end to the bumper of a pickup. Dozens of rusting and wrecked cars and trucks surrounded the mechanic's work space. The man didn't even look up as I maneuvered around piles of salvaged auto parts and down a lane toward the rear of the property where a small, square adobe stood in the center of clean ground.

"This is it," Charlie said. "The door's open. Either somebody's at home or somebody had been here."

We got out. Charlie called out a greeting in Spanish to see if anyone was there. Neither of us knew who or what to expect. One of Barrilito's sons or even a stranger might have taken over the house. In Mexico, few buildings, however humble, remain empty. Nor was this one. As soon as Charlie heard a woman's voice answer, he stepped aside and let me go first.

"Señora," I called, "may we speak with you?"

The voice gave us permission to come inside.

I went first. The light from a window opposite the door gave the one room its only illumination. All four walls were papered with black-and-white photographs. The scant furnishings included a single table turned into a home altar. Objects crowded the cloth-covered surface. Among them were a statue of the Madonna with a rosary dangling from the clasped hands, a toy horse, two candles stuck in Coke bottles, and a plastic infant Jesus. In the corner, a low cupboard provided storage space for both dishes and clothes. Curled up in the one chair was a Chihuahua wearing a knitted jacket to keep it warm. The other occupant was the pregnant young woman from the funeral, who was seated on a narrow bed pushed against the right-hand wall. Her body looked thin and shrunken against the swell of the impending birth. The air in the room was stuffy and her face glistened with sweat. She had dark skin, a wide face, and the thoughtful, sweet manner of many Mexican women, beneath which lay a strength of character and will that was the backbone of the Mexican family.

"Do you remember me?" I asked. "We sat next to each other at the service for Señor Soto." I introduced Charlie.

She nodded shyly, and said, "I am Pachá. Have you come to put me out of the house?" She spoke slowly, as if the baby soon to be born had pushed the breath out of her.

"No, we have nothing to do with the house. I was told it was Señor Soto's property and I wanted to speak to anyone who might be here," I said, making up the story as I went along. "I hoped to perhaps buy some of his photographs." If necessary I would make good on the lie. I could hardly admit I had hoped to find the place empty and snoop around.

She looked pained. "Vicente said he would take care of me," Pachá said, "but now he's dead and it's *la vida mala* for me."

La vida mala. The bad life. That meant she had no other home, no family to support her, and would be on the street.

"Those *ingratos*, his sons, would not recognize me at the funeral, but only two days before they came here and took away all Vicente's possessions, his clothes, his Bible, even his shaving things. And what that old woman called me, it's not true. I am not a *puta*. Never have I sold myself." Tears welled in her eyes and she put her hand on her heavy stomach. "I must not get sick with anger and grief. My child will drink it in."

"Pachá, did Señor Soto have many visitors here or travel to Presidio often?"

"He worked the *zócalo* only, many hours. He sold most of the pictures to tourists. Since I have been here the only visitor has been Señora Garza, the beautician I swept the floor for before I met Vicente. Maybe after the baby is born, I go back to work for her."

"May we look at the photographs on the wall?" I asked.

She nodded. "Vicente was kind and he took good care of me. He paid in advance for the midwife for my delivery." She took a deep breath and released it in a long, soft sigh. "He said everything was going to change for us. He said he would buy a fine new camera and take pictures of rich people."

Though the prints were not the best quality, the photographs had been taken by a man with an eye for balance, line, and subject. Soto had been, after all, an artist of sorts. Most were of *nortéamericanos*, many were scenes of daily life in the town. I scanned the walls for some clue to a photograph that might have somehow gotten Barrilito killed, but found nothing significant, except an empty spot with a snippet of the torn-away photograph attached.

"What was here?" I asked.

"A picture of some men. The blue-eyed Mexican who came here to tell me Vicente was dead took it."

"Blue-eyed . . . when was he here? Do you remember?"

She pointed to the wall calendar on which each day had been carefully marked off. "The midwife said I should mark off the days of my pregnancy. I put a little check for when the man came."

The calendar had a bright picture of three Mexican women and had been a *farmacia* giveaway. The tiny check mark was on the Wednesday after the first weekend of November, the weekend when Clay and Fran and I had been at the Marfa Lights Festival.

"Pachá, did the man say why he wanted this particular photograph?"

"No. He pulled it down and gave me five dollars. I told him he could take all he wanted, but that was the only one. It was the other man in the uniform that took away all the negatives. He said it was police business. That he might find the man who killed Vicente from his pictures. I asked him why he did not take the pictures and he said he would make new ones from the negatives. I don't think the police care who killed Vicente. Why should they? He wasn't rich or important. I don't understand why these men came here or Vicente's sons. They searched everything with their eyes."

"Did Señor Soto ever say anything to you about getting money for his photographs from anyone on the other side? Or someone here in town? Someone influential."

"You are thinking *la droga*. No. I don't say that if such temptations came his way . . ." She shifted slightly on the bed, as if trying to find a comfortable position.

"Are there other photographs, some he might have stored away?"

"Maybe his sons have some. I don't know. I didn't know about the others of his family until a little before the funeral." She started to say something more, then her skin paled and she cried out, "Pain! I have much pain."

I ran to her side. "What is it? What's wrong?"

"Oh, something is bad with the baby!"

"We'll take you to the hospital."

"No hospital. The midwife is paid. The midwife is supposed to be here." She was crying now. She tried to get up and I helped her to her feet. Where she had been sitting the mattress was wet with blood.

"*Cálmase*," I told her. "Be calm. We're going to the hospital."

She clenched my hand hard, bit her lip, and nodded agreement.

Charlie said, "I'll pull the pickup right up to the door." When he came back in, he put his arm around her and together we got her to the pickup. "Lean on the side here, until I get something," Charlie said. He ran back inside and came out carrying the mattress under one arm, the chair in the other hand. He threw the mattress into the back end, lowered the tailgate, placed the chair beneath it, and told Pachá to sit down. Together, we hoisted woman and chair onto the tailgate. I climbed up and helped her out of the chair and onto the mattress. She lay moaning while I held her hand. The drive across town to the city hospital near the bridge seemed to take forever.

By the time we reached the hospital, Pachá was worse, her legs thrashing as I held her shoulders. As Charlie ran inside and emerged with a man in a jumpsuit pushing a gurney, a Jeep pulled in behind us. Charlie lifted Pachá onto the gurney while the hospital worker steadied it. As I jumped down to help, a burly man got out of the Jeep and followed us into the hospital. We followed the clattering gurney down a long corridor until an old nurse held up her hand and commanded Charlie and me to stop. "Only family inside," she said, looking at me questioningly. With my dark hair and olive skin I am often taken for a Mexican. I shook my head and the nurse motioned us back with her hands. Swinging doors closed behind Pachá.

When we turned around, the cop was right behind us. A large-caliber pistol rode his hip and his jackboots had been polished to a high gloss. A stripe marked each side of his tight pants, khaki like his shirt that was open at the neck, showing the curly black hair on his chest in contrast to his hairless, polished skull. The police have to buy their own guns. The pistol had a pearl handle. Here was a man successful in taking bribes.

"*Policia,*" he said. "You ran three red lights of our city. Would you do that in Texas?"

I knew the drill. "Is there some way to resolve this so that we may wait here to see if our friend is all right?" I said, reaching into my pocket. I pulled out a five dollar bill and placed it on his open palm. Two dollars would have been enough for one red light.

He looked at it, then me, palm still up. "Traffic safety is so important, don't you agree." I added another five. He smiled and folded the cash away in his breast pocket. "A pleasure to do business with you. Officer Gregorio Esparza, at your service. Your friend is a tourist? May I help in any way with translation?"

We had been speaking in English. I switched to Spanish, telling him our friend was a local woman we had been visiting when she had a serious medical complication and we didn't have time to wait for an ambulance.

The double doors behind squeaked open and we turned around to see a tired man in a soiled white jacket over poor quality clothes.

"In that case, señora," Officer Esparza said, as the doctor approached, "your kindness to one of our citizens is appreciated." He returned my money with a sharp salute and a brilliant smile.

With a glance at Esparza, the doctor said, "There is a complication. I have to anesthetize her for surgery. Is there family here to give consent?"

I explained that as far as we knew Pachá had no family.

"This is a problem. Someone *must* give consent."

There did not seem to be a choice. I told him to do whatever was necessary.

"By giving permission, if anything happens, you are acting as guardian. It is conceivable that she could die. You are liable." He turned away and pushed back through the double doors. A nurse stepped forward with papers for me to sign. No one asked for the patient's name.

"Do not worry," Officer Esparza said cheerfully. "That one mostly knows what he's doing. Here is my card. Should there be any trouble for you, present this and the police will disturb you no further. Adios."

I'd seen a lot of strange things in Mexico, but a policeman with business cards was a new one. I put the cheaply printed card away in my billfold.

We sat on a hard, wooden bench in the hallway, staring at the scarred linoleum floor with dirt packed in the cracks. There were no framed prints on the wall, no lamps, only the stark tube light in the ceiling. Through the open door of an empty room, I saw bloody bandages on the floor.

Finally the doctor came out. "She'll sleep for hours."

"Is she all right? What about the baby?"

"A girl. Very small."

I took a pencil and paper from my pocket, printed the name Roberto Soto, and handed it to the doctor. "This is the name of the person to get in touch with about the hospital bill," I told him. I thought that one of the Soto sons might as well be involved. They could spend some of their father's cash on Pachá. I had expected him to ask me to pay the bill right there, but the salute of Officer Esparza must have had its effect on the good doctor.

"She'll need clothes," the doctor said, pocketing the paper. "We had to cut off what she was wearing."

Back in the pickup I made a U-turn on the street and drove back to the adobe. The shirtless man, hands black with grime, was still bent over the motor. This time, he stood upright as we turned in, waved us over, and asked, "Is the girl okay? Is it the baby?"

We explained what had happened. I asked if he

would look after Pachá's dog until she came home and he agreed.

Charlie waited in the pickup as I went inside. The Chihuahua raised his head, but didn't bark. I found some dried dog food and filled his bowl. The water bowl was full. I opened the cupboard and selected some clothes. The only thing I could find to put them in was a brown paper bag. As I folded the garments, I noticed through the window an outhouse behind the adobe. Pachá's outdoor toilet would be cleaner, I thought, than the hospital's bathroom. I carried the bag out to the pickup, handed it through the window to Charlie, and told him I needed to visit the facility around back. "Watch out for spiders," he said.

I slipped the latch and stepped inside. Here, too, Barrilito had papered the walls with his photographs. One instantly caught my eye because I knew the man and woman in it. Barrilito's old camera had captured an image of lust and coquetry. I broke a fingernail removing the tack and taking down the photograph. I felt stupid. A blue-eyed Mexican, Pachá had said. Rano Johnson. Could this photograph of him and Cosmé Crosswell be a copy of the one he had given Pachá five dollars for?

I rejoined Charlie, showing him what I'd found. He whistled, said, "Damnation, she made a *cabrón* out of Howie."

Cabrón literally means billy goat. Used as Charlie had, in Mexico it meant a man with an unfaithful wife. Barrilito had photographed the deputy and Cosmé, arms entwined, standing in the doorway of an Ojinaga hotel.

We dropped the clothes off at the hospital, trying unsuccessfully to find anyone who could tell me anything about Pachá or her baby.

Back in the pickup, Charlie wanted to talk. "I guess we know now why Johnson took the photograph from the house. It must have been another one of these," he said, tapping the photograph.

I had other things on my mind as I raced for the border and the first public rest room I could find. In the shock of finding the photograph of Rano Johnson cozying up to Cosmé I had forgotten to use the outdoor toilet.

The rest of the drive home was uneventful. Clay's vetmobile, parked by the clinic, had been freshly washed. He was in the shower singing mightily, something he did only when he thought no one was there to hear. Charlie grinned at me and ambled into the front. I went into the bedroom and stuck my head around the bathroom door to tell Clay we were home. All song ceased. I put the photo down on the table, washed my hands, poured three whiskeys, and invited Charlie back to the living area. He sat on the couch, Phobe scrambled onto his lap, and I took my chair near the fireplace. In short order, Clay, his hair damp, his jeans and shirt fresh, joined us.

"If ever I saw two people who looked guilty of something, it's you two."

By the time Charlie and I told our story, we had

each downed two short whiskeys and emptied a bowl of peanuts.

"So, the very married Rano Johnson is across the border with the very married Cosmé Crosswell," Clay said, looking at the photograph in his hand.

"Rano Johnson is married, too?" I said. "How do you know that?"

"He wears a wedding band," Clay said.

"That may explain why he pretended not to know anything about Barrilito right after the murder," I said.

Charlie said, "Most times, Mexicans don't volunteer information about each other to strangers. Johnson was crazy to take a chance like that just to get that photograph. If the Mexican police knew that a Texas deputy was doing the law's business on their side, even informing the next of kin, they'd be kicking him back to this side with a formal complaint to his boss and anybody else they could think of."

"It must have been very important to him, then, to risk it," I said.

"Have you thought what this photograph might mean for Howie?" Clay said.

"What do you mean?" I said.

"It may strengthen the case against him. With a rocky marriage, he may have figured he had nothing to lose by murdering Row."

"I have no reason to show it to anyone. I took it from the wall on impulse."

Later, just as Clay and I were turning out the lights, the telephone rang. Phobe raised her head and cast a look of disdain at the noise. She dislikes anything that makes sudden and loud sounds. Clay answered. His part of the conversation consisted of short answers.

"Who was that?" I asked as soon as he hung up.

"Leila Spivey. She wants to see me in the morning."

I turned out the light and closed my eyes, but I couldn't stop myself from speculating about Leila. Finally I asked, "Did she say why she wanted to see you?"

All I got for an answer was a snore.

SEVENTEEN

Early the next morning I stood outside in the cold air, my hands stuffed in my pockets, pondering the wisdom of my intentions while watching Phobe sniff the air and follow a scent through the desert scrub behind Clay's office. With her head cocked, the bobcat used her paw to poke at something I could not see but that she detected by its scent.

Phobe walked up to me proudly holding something in her mouth, then dropped her prey at my feet. The tiny cactus mouse, all huge eyes and hairless tail, remained perfectly still, instinctively aware that any move would catch the predator's quick eye and bring down tooth and claw. I praised Phobe and cooed over her gift, then scooping the terrified mouse into my hand and clutching it lightly, I carried it off to the brush and placed it on the ground. It took a moment to realize its freedom, then swiveled and darted for cover.

Both Phobe and I were ready to go inside. The bobcat had had her fun and I had come to a decision. I fed Phobe and while she ate, I telephoned Cosmé Crosswell.

Three hours later, I was helping three little boys choose between candy and Joya tamarind soft drinks when Cosmé came through the door and down the center aisle, her thick hair bouncing rhythmically with her long strides. She wore a tunic of pale yellow and a long, red skirt with black boots. Two Mexican nationals buying plastic pipe fittings eyed her appreciatively as they left. The children paid and left quickly. The door had not slammed behind the boy's running feet when Cosmé said, "This had better be important. I was supposed to meet with Howie's lawyer this morning."

"I wanted to ask you about this," I said, taking Barrilito's photograph from the shelf beneath the counter and placing it on top where she could see it.

She glanced down at it. I had expected her face to show at least embarrassment. I saw only genuine puzzlement. "Where did you get that?" she asked, transferring her look to me.

Rather than answer her question, I asked one of mine own. "When was it taken?"

"A few months ago. June I think, or maybe May."

"Who took it?"

"Some street photographer in OJ."

"You don't know his name?"

Cosmé made an impatient noise. "He was a street vendor. There are dozens of those people peddling everything from shoe shines to pastries. They don't introduce themselves. He snapped the picture, then asked us to pay and promised he'd print a copy and have it back to us in an hour."

"Did you pay him?"

"Rano did. He paid him five dollars. I told him he was wasting his money because that camera was so old the picture would probably be terrible, but Rano said he wanted a picture of us together. Where did you get it?"

I answered her with another question of my own. "Did you know that the man who took this was the man who was murdered on the road right outside my front door?"

"I didn't even know anybody had been murdered except that old man they say Howie killed. I've had troubles of my own, you know."

"Look, Cosmé, why don't you come back to the kitchen where we can sit down and be comfortable."

She swept a hand through her hair and said, "I drove all this way. I might as well."

I led the way through, closing the door between the front and our living quarters so we wouldn't be interrupted. Cosmé arranged herself on the couch. Her self-awareness seemed total. Had there been a mirror in the room, she would have been watching herself in it, as if she were directing a scene in which she starred.

I poured coffee into the waiting cups, placed the tray on the worn bench that served as both coffee table and footstool, and excused myself to telephone Charlie, who waited in Clay's office, taking messages and referring emergencies to Leila's telephone number. I told him my guest had arrived and asked if he would take the front counter for me. Charlie was tactful. From the window, I saw him walk past, going around to the front in order not to disturb us.

I put sweet rolls on plates and joined my guest. She had poured almost as much half-and-half into her coffee as I like in mine and had finished the sweet roll. I handed her my untouched plate and she smiled for the first time, a little half-embarrassed grin. "Thanks. I didn't eat breakfast."

I let her finish her food, then asked, "Tell me about you and Howie, Cosmé. What happened?"

She sat in complete repose, no nervous looks or gestures. How could Howie have resisted painting her? Her voice was calm when she started to speak.

"*Mamá* was fond of old sayings, Mexican *dichos*. She had one for everything. When I was twelve or thirteen, and boys started to notice me, she told me, 'My daughter, in love first comes the honey, then the hard bread of bitterness.' " She lifted her chin. "I showed Howie that I had sharp-pointed teeth to bite that hard bread. For the first year everything was good. Then he started drinking again. We fought a lot. He had no respect for me. I think he wanted to humiliate me because I am Mexican. He wanted his dead Anglo wife, the little *güera*, the one he painted every day. I told him, if you wanted a blonde, why did you marry me? He was a real *borrachín* by that time, always a bottle in his hand. All that drink made him weak so that with his own wife he could not be a *hombre de verdad*. So I shamed him and found a real man."

"Rano Johnson."

"I've known him all my life. He always liked me, but he didn't have enough ambition. Even in high school, I knew what I wanted, to have my own ranch. He wanted to be the sheriff of this county someday. No one who wears an honest badge makes the kind of money it takes to buy land. So when he asked to marry me, I said no way. I started seeing him again last year after he promised me he'd get me a ranch. He said he'd leave his wife and kids and he wanted me to leave Howie then, but I told him, no, promises don't count. He had to prove to me he could get enough money for the land first." She rubbed one finger across her wedding ring. "Now that Howie has been arrested, I'll do my duty and stay with him through his trial. Then I'll divorce him. When that happens, if Rano can get me what I want, I'll marry him. If not . . ." She shrugged dismissively.

"You gave him an ultimatum?"

"I told him it was over between us unless he improved his situation soon. He knew what that meant. I wasn't going to wait much longer."

"Has Rano ever said anything to you about this photograph, or mentioned Vicente Soto? That's the name of the street photographer. His nickname was Barrilito."

"I never heard Rano say either name."

"How often did you and Rano go across to Ojinaga?"

"Two or three times a month, maybe. We'd meet on the square in the evenings, have dinner, then stay overnight at the Hotel Rohana. Other times, Rano would come to my house for a few hours."

She made no pretense of being ashamed of her behavior. Indeed, she seemed pleased to be talking about it, her pragmatic attitude toward money was a source of pride, her affair with Johnson a necessity as much as a pleasure.

"He wasn't worried that Howie would see him?"

"Howie lived in his studio. All he did was paint and drink. The only time he came into the house was when he wanted to shower or eat. And if he'd seen us together it wouldn't have mattered. He knew I'd taken a lover because I told him. He said I had no shame." She shrugged. "The shame was his, not mine, the *cabrón*. A man who can't please his wife is no man at all."

There was a knock at the door and Charlie came in and announced Sheriff Tate, who followed on his heels. "Ladies," he said, removing his hat, "I'm sorry to interrupt."

"I was just going," Cosmé said, rising.

"It's you I've come to see, Mrs. Crosswell," the sheriff said. "Your husband's lawyer said you mentioned you'd be here. I'm sorry to tell you, but Mr. Crosswell tried to hang himself in his cell."

I couldn't see Cosmé's face, but her body swayed back slightly away from the sheriff. Then she said, "I'll go to the hospital." Tate offered to drive her and send someone back for her truck, but she was already moving toward the door. He followed her and Charlie and I walked behind them and watched as Cosmé and Tate drove away in separate vehicles. A customer drove up and Charlie said he'd take care of him. I went back to the living area and locked the photograph away in the desk drawer.

The back door burst open and Clay came bounding in saying, "You'll never guess what the Spivey sisters have proposed doing with their estate." He circled the room, talking excitedly. "They're going to fund scholarships in veterinary medicine at Texas A & M. Each recipient will be required to spend the first year after graduation working in Presidio. There'll be a foundation to be headquartered at the ranch, which will be used for sick or abused horses."

I didn't want to break into his happiness with the news about Howie Crosswell. I said, "Clay, that's wonderful."

"It gets better. They've asked me to be on the foundation's board. I'll be responsible for working with the university to select the recipients and supervise them when they graduate. This means Presidio will have a vet and I'll have some help. And it won't hurt our finances one bit, either."

"Leila must really feel guilty about feeding you that peyote," I said.

He laughed. "I forgive her. I'll even tear up their bill for treating the cattle."

"Don't be too hasty. We have the monthly note on the vetmobile to think about. Besides, they might change their minds."

"They've already contacted a lawyer. The university is sending the development officer out next week with the forms to establish the Randall and Florence Spivey Scholarship in Veterinary Medicine."

"Clay, I am glad."

He rubbed his hands together. "Maybe I can talk the sisters into funding free vaccinations for dogs and cats. Now, what's been happening here?"

Before I could answer, Charlie came in saying, "You had a message about—" he fished in his pockets and found a slip of paper "—a horse with bad breath, and he fights the bit."

Clay took the note from Charlie's hand and got up, saying, "Dental problem." He looked at the address. "I'll have a sandwich and go."

"Sit down," I told him. "I'll get the sandwiches."

Over the hasty meal, I told Clay about Howie. We didn't have time to discuss it. No one eats faster than Clay when he knows an animal needs help. While he was gone, between customers, I told Charlie about my conversation with Cosmé.

"Poor Howie. So he did know about them. Maybe that's why he tried to kill himself," he said.

Just at closing time, a rancher came in. His pickup had a broken water hose and he'd walked in from down the road. I had the part and Charlie drove him back to his vehicle.

I sat on the porch, the light off, looking at the stars and enjoying the quiet. I thought about how many people we knew who had spent their lives on the border yet refused to cross into Ojinaga. "Too dangerous," most said. "If the food poisoning doesn't get you, the lead poisoning will," one man told me, referring to the lawlessness that prevailed. Yet here was a deputy sheriff who had gone to the border city to conduct his romance with another man's wife. For a lawman, it was doubly chancy. I knew how the border worked as well as Rano Johnson did. Had he visited Ojinaga for another reason, using his affair with Cosmé as an excuse? Had that reason been serious enough for him to kill to keep it quiet? Adultery and divorce wouldn't have gotten the deputy fired. Roberto Soto had told me that his father never went anywhere without his camera. Maybe the photograph Johnson had removed from Barrilito's house hadn't been the same one I found in the outhouse. Maybe it had been one that would send Johnson to prison. Maybe that was how Barrilito had gotten the cash his sons had been spending, having found it hidden among the things they had taken from his house. I had the deputy's badge. What if, instead of losing it, as I had thought, Barrilito had torn it off as Rano shot him.

I looked up to see that Charlie had returned. He sat on the steps, his sneakers tapping against the wood. "I've been thinking," he said, "about that Rano Johnson and Howie's wife. He wants her. She wants the prestige of money and land. I can only think of one way that he could give her what she wants. I think the sheriff is right. Drug smuggling is involved in Barrilito's murder, only he's got the wrong person in mind. As I see it, that has to be what Johnson is doing." Charlie turned around and looked at me. "I think you'd better tell the sheriff everything Cosmé told you and give him that photograph."

EIGHTEEN

Sunday morning brought gusty desert winds and sunlight so bright in the spotless sky that the shadows cast by boulders and scrub looked as black as India ink. A busload of pilgrims from across the river had arrived to keep vigil beneath the image of Our Lady of the Trading Post. Charlie had left after breakfast intending to visit Howie in the hospital.

In sleepless moments during the night, I had worried over my suspicions about Rano Johnson. Was I seeing guilt where there was merely coincidence, or were such seeming coincidences a trail of facts leading to more than one crime, if what I thought was true? Sometime before dawn I had arrived at a conclusion, based on fatigue as much as logic. When in doubt, wait.

Clay and I spent the long, slow morning hours reading. As well as the Presidio newspaper, we subscribe to the *Big Bend Sentinel,* published in Marfa. Clay read the *Sentinel*'s front page coverage of the Marfa Shorthorns football team's defeat of the Presidio Blue Devils, 52-20. I read *The International*'s story about thefts of bulldozers the past week from three more ranches.

"Clay, listen to this," I said, reading part of the article aloud. " 'According to Deputy Dennis Bustamente, each ranch where equipment has been stolen had either an absentee owner or the owner was away from home at the time, making it likely that someone was involved who knew not only the maze of ranch roads crisscrossing the county, but the habits and plans of the ranchers. It would be worth a lot of cash to someone to have an informed spotter. The Sheriff's Department is reminding landowners to notify it whenever they plan to be away so they can give more attention to where the thieves might strike next.' " I closed the newspaper. "Who better to be a spotter for thieves than a deputy."

"Dennis? Come on, Texana," Clay said. "That's impossible." He ducked his head back into his own reading.

"Not Dennis. Rano Johnson." I told Clay about Charlie's belief that the deputy had to be involved in drug smuggling. "It could be more than that. Maybe he's a spotter for any sort of crime involving both sides of the river. Equipment disappearing into Mexico, drug runners or illegals needing to know which ranches are safe to cross, where the patrols are going to be, who's on the checkpoints on a given day, all that."

"Slow down and take a breath," Clay said. "That's a plausible theory, but the sheriff isn't likely to jump on it with both feet, you know."

"There have been plenty of law enforcement people who worked the border regions on this side, including two sheriffs that I can think of, who have been arrested and charged with either drug smuggling or taking bribes from drug kingpins. It's easy to take the high road until somebody shoves a bag of money under your nose. I'm tired of us being in the eye of suspicion. If the sheriff says one more word to me about Barrilito's murder, I'll give him something else to think about."

Clay put his newspaper on the table and stood up as we heard a car door slam out front. He went through to the front and came back with the sheriff in tow, winking at me before he turned to motion Tate to a chair. "What brings you all this way?"

The sheriff picked up a chair, turned it the wrong way round, threw his leg over like a rider mounting a pony, and sat with his arms resting along the top of the back.

"How'd the funeral go? Nice crowd?" he asked, unsmiling.

"You should have been there," Clay said. "Except for us, it was all family."

I said, "Did the Border Patrol tell you where we were?"

Tate said, "I see your man, this Cadillac Charlie character, mentioned the boys visited here. He gets around a lot, doesn't he. Crossed over to Ojinaga with you, Mrs. Jones. You seem to be visiting the other side more than usual lately."

I unlocked the desk drawer, lifted out Barrilito's photograph of Johnson and Cosmé, and handed it to the sheriff. "I found that at Barrilito's place. You mentioned my visiting the other side as if it was a crime. Rano Johnson has been visiting the other side, including a visit to the murdered photographer's house to get a photograph."

"This one?" he asked.

"I don't know what photograph he took," I said. "It might have been a copy of this, it might have been something else altogether. Maybe you should look closer to home for the person who murdered Barrilito."

Tate's face gave away nothing, but when he stopped staring at the photograph, he placed it carefully on the seat of a nearby chair, raised a hand, and said, "First Mrs. Jones," counting on his fingers, "Deputy Johnson is one of the most competent lawmen I've ever been acquainted with. Second, as far as I know, he's happily married, with good kids that he loves. Third, he works long hours, many of them without pay. I call that dedication."

I was beginning to wish he'd run out of fingers.

"Four, I know he rubs some people the wrong way, but that's the nature of the job. You show me a photograph of my deputy with his arm around a woman who's not his wife, toss out some serious accusations, and expect me to buy a ticket for railroading—"

"That's exactly what you've done in regard to my wife, Sheriff," Clay said. "Hear me out. We had a man we didn't know murdered out front and you immediately infer that we're involved. You questioned our neighbors, our friends, my wife's customers, threatened to park the Border Patrol outside to cut off business from the other side, and made a hell of a long drive on a Sunday morning to question us because we went to a funeral in Ojinaga. Don't talk to my wife about jumping to conclusions. I have as fine an opinion of her, and so do the folks around here, as you do of your deputy. If you want to track down the real killer of Barrilito, you're following the wrong scent."

I thought it was time for me to intervene. "Look, Sheriff, I'm only asking you to think about all this. That's fair, isn't it? Talk to Cosmé Crosswell yourself and ask her about Johnson. Show that photograph to him and see what he says."

"With respect, ma'am, I know my job." Tate extricated himself from his seat and picked up the photograph. He touched his hand to his hat and bid us good-bye.

Clay and I ate a late lunch of baked potatoes and salad, then stretched out on the bed with Phobe for a nap.

When Charlie came back at six, Clay and I had just finished watching a video. We asked him how Howie Crosswell was doing.

Charlie sat down on the couch and clasped his hands together. "He's recovering. The hospital expects to release him back into custody tomorrow. I told him about that photograph. He didn't act surprised."

"Cosmé said he knew about her affair with Johnson," I said.

Charlie said, "Nearly dying seems to have done Howie some good. He's in a fighting mood now, ready to defend himself against the murder charge. He fired the lawyer Cosmé and Miss Leila got for him. The lawyer wanted him to take a plea bargain from murder to manslaughter because of the gun being found in the studio. So my question is, do you know a good criminal lawyer?"

I looked at Clay, who said, "We don't know a good one. We know a great one. Whether he'll take the case or not, well, we'll have to talk to someone about that. Texana, call Fran."

I protested. "Jake is too expensive—"

"I have a pension," Charlie said, "and I never spend it, I just invest, and reinvest the earnings. I can pay."

I looked at Charlie with fresh eyes, thinking that maybe the nickname Cadillac Charlie was more apt than I had known. "She's *your* sister," I said to Clay. "Why don't you talk to her?"

"It's easier to say no to a brother. She and Jake,

well, we don't know how she'll feel about his coming here, you know."

I knew. I called. Just saying hello, Fran sounded happy.

I skipped over the pleasantries.

"Do you read the local paper?"

"No. It's been blissful, not keeping up with anything but the plans for the gallery, and now the house."

"I asked because I thought you might have read about the charges against Howie Crosswell."

"I don't have to read the paper for that, Texana," Fran said. "It's all anybody in town is talking about."

"He needs a lawyer, a really good one—"

"You want Jake?" Fran said at the same time.

"Yes, and our friend Charlie says he'll take care of Jake's fees. Howie doesn't have much."

Charlie nodded.

"Tell your friend Charlie that if he wants Jake the operative word is bleed, not pay."

I put my hand over the receiver and said to Charlie, "She says it will be very expensive." He gave me an okay sign.

I said, "It's just Jake's kind of case, Fran. Look what happened to Howie, his wife and kids killed, this man gets—"

"I know. It has what Jake calls the three P's: poignancy, pity, and publicity. He'll have twenty motions filed before the local district attorney has gee-whizzed his way through his first television interview. Want me to call Jake now?"

"Would you?" I said, giving Charlie a thumbs-up.

"I have a selfish motive in wanting Jake to take this case," she said. "I've bought a house in Marfa. Jake has agreed to cut back on his practice. He's promised to fly out on weekends until he can finish up his present caseload, then we'll get to know each other again and see how things go. I've thought all along he would be great on Crosswell's case, but the man already had a lawyer. This is perfect from my point of view. It gets Jake out here and committed. It will keep him here long enough to learn to like the place, if he's going to."

"Tell her if Mr. Dare says yes, I can wire a deposit to his bank," Charlie whispered.

I repeated his words to Fran.

"Oh, he'll say yes," she said. "If I can get 'round his answering machine, I'll talk to him and call you back." She hung up. It seemed the adrenaline of murder was pumping some energy into Fran's flagging marriage.

My sister-in-law, I thought, had needed a change, not from Jake, but from herself. She'd found it and I was glad for her.

For a little more than an hour we waited, jumping nervously when the telephone rang. I answered, mouthing to Charlie and Clay, "It's Fran."

"He'll fly out day after tomorrow and talk to Howie Crosswell, but I can tell he's already smelling headlines, a book deal, and a made-for-television movie. About fees, tell your friend Charlie to stand mute. Jake already has more money than he can spend. He can do this pro bono. It will make a great hook for the media when he announces that he took the case because he believed Howie was suffering an injustice even being charged."

We hung up and I told Charlie the good news.

"This is a good evening's work. I owe you guys for this," Charlie said.

"If Howie didn't do it, who did?" I asked.

"That's the question, isn't it," Charlie said, "even if Mr. Dare gets him off."

Charlie went to wash the Cadillac. He took Phobe with him because she loves to play in the water, any water, hose, bathtub. She likes to shower with me when I'll let her. Clay joked about his sister learning to love the desert, but I could tell he was pleased at the idea that she might stay on in Marfa. The remainder of the day was pleasantly uneventful and I had lots of time to think. That is what always gets me in trouble.

NINETEEN

*S*leep would not come. I lay in bed, one hand touching the warm fur of Phobe's head, listening to Clay's irregular breathing, a sign he was dreaming, possibly heading into a nightmare. I seldom dream and when I do I remember nothing of the details, unlike Clay, who recalls his nightmares with clarity.

I turned on my side and stared through the window into the silvery night, watching the moon appear to shrink as it rose beyond the magnifying effect of the earth's atmosphere. I could not stop thinking about Ella Spivey and Julian Row dancing on the road with a bottle of champagne cooling on the hood of the car. Why did someone buy champagne except to celebrate?

Fran had told me that when she arrived at the municipal airport in Alpine, she had seen Row and Ella. Had they been picking someone up, saying good-bye to someone, or departing themselves? Only private planes used the small airport. It should be easy to check and find out whether Row and Ella had chartered a flight and if so, to what destination.

Then there was Leila and her ease handling guns and horses, thanks to "Daddy's" tutoring, her attitude toward predators, as she had referred to Row, and her admitted attempt to drug Ella's beau with peyote and the desperation that implied. Leila had character traits I admired: her independence, her mastery of the ranching way of life, even to some degree her ruthlessness, a characteristic I had my own share of. Countering that, I recognized the manipulativeness inherent in her domination over her sisters and the arrogance behind her uninvited intrusion into Howie Crosswell's life and problems.

I closed my eyes. The next thing I knew, I heard the birds twittering in the flush of dawn. I sat up. The covers on Clay's side of the bed were thrown back, the dent where Phobe had slept between us marked with hairs from her fur.

From the kitchen, I smelled bacon and eggs and in minutes Clay brought in breakfast on a tray.

I had eaten and returned the tray to the kitchen when Fran called, inviting me to see her house in Marfa and to help her select the paint colors for the walls. Putting down the telephone, I went to ask Clay his plans for the day. He had no pressing appointments, no ranch visits scheduled. It would be no trouble for him to keep an eye on things and Charlie was there if needed. I told Fran to expect me in four hours. I showered, dressed, and left for Marfa, looking forward to the day. I'm a frustrated decorator, spending hours going over house magazines and planning rooms I don't have. Our living quarters are small, even for two people.

Under the blue sky, Marfa's low buildings shone in soft, ice-cream colors of pink, cream, and white. I drove as Fran had directed me to Jeff Davis Street and parked at the curb in front of a once-grand two-story adobe with a FOR SALE sign with a SOLD sticker taped over it. An arch-covered walkway led to a side door that opened into a sun room, its row of windows cloudy with dust. I called Fran's name and heard a voice from above and hurrying footsteps as she came down the corner staircase far enough to peek at me and say, "Come up here," before retreating.

"Up here" was a deep landing repeating the window pattern of the room below. "This is bigger than our living quarters," I said, rubbing the dust from one window to see the long view of the mountains, and below, what once must have been a graveled, desert garden, one that belonged in our dry climate and fitted the southwestern architecture of the house.

"Trost, the same architect that build the Paisano, designed this," Fran said proudly. She stood in a circle of paint cans, brushing another color on the interior wall and standing back to inspect a patchwork of varied colors. "Which do you like?"

"The peach color."

She shook her head. "Not complementary with enough other colors. I want to hang art on this wall. I may go for yellow. It's dramatic, don't you think?"

"What type of art will you hang?"

"Whatever I like, as long as it's fresh and not western. I don't want it to look like a duplicate of the Espuela Foundation display. This should reflect our gallery. Picasso and I have decided to call it simply Beens-Dare Gallery."

I spent three hours with Fran, going from room to room, trying colors, turning the thick pages of wallpaper sample books, and holding fabric swatches up to paint samples. We ate a picnic-style lunch on the cracked stones of the patio while Fran told me her design plans for the grounds.

By unconscious intent, I took the scenic route home and instead of passing the cutoff to the seven sisters' ranch, I turned in, realizing that all along I'd wanted to see Leila in order to test my nighttime theories by light of day and determine whether they would hold up. I bumped up the road, making good time on the rough track, but doing the shocks no favors.

I knew something was wrong as soon as I reached the house and saw the front door standing open. Before I stopped, Clara came running to meet me.

"I'm so glad you're here. Maybe you can talk some sense into Leila. Come in, come in."

"What's going on?" I asked, following Clara's scurrying figure into the house.

"Leila's lost her mind, that's what," Clara said.

In the living room, her sisters stood clustered around Leila, who sat with clamped, bloodless lips, her arms folded tightly across her chest, her face set in an expression of mute stubbornness except for the searing glance she gave me when Clara announced, "Texana Jones is here. Maybe you'll listen to her."

Mattie's old face held an expression of hurt. Viola cried into a tea towel and even Hattie looked shaken. Clearly they'd had a shock, but what? I waited for someone to tell me what was going on.

Clara broke the ranks of silence. "We wanted to call the sheriff, but Leila wouldn't let us."

Leila's head snapped up. "Shut your mouth, Clara Spivey. Not another word. Not a sound from any of you, do you hear me?"

"I won't be quiet," Clara said in a loud voice. "That's the trouble with us. We've been too damned quiet all our lives." Her hand, trembling with her anger, flew to cover her lips at the unaccustomed profanity, but she quickly recovered. "That man threatened you. He had a gun. Don't deny it. I saw it. I thought he was going to shoot you, then come in the house and kill all of us. You gave him an envelope and you won't say what was in it. We want to know what's going on."

"You don't know what you're saying, Clara," Leila said. Her angry eyes swept her sisters' faces. "There's not two cents' worth of sense in your five heads. Do the math."

"What man?" I said.

Leila and Clara both spoke at once, the one trying to stop the other. Clara got out the name Rano Johnson even as Hattie grabbed her arm and tried to shush her. At Clara's words, Leila pressed a hand to her eyes. Hattie dropped her hold on Clara's arm and let her square shoulders slump.

Clara seized the opportunity. "He came here to see Leila—"

"—he asked for her," Sarah said.

Clara said, "She went outside to talk to him and he shouted at her and he had his hand on the gun. She came back inside and went to her room and came out with an envelope and took it to him. Then he drove off."

"Leila," I said sharply. "Is Johnson headed to Mexico? Why did he threaten you? What happened?"

"There was money in that envelope," Viola said loudly, flinging aside the tea towel. "I was with her when she withdrew it from the bank."

"Mind your own business," Leila said, holding tightly to both arms of the chair as if restraining herself from jumping at her sister.

I didn't have time to ponder why the stubborn old woman was so determined to help Rano Johnson get away.

Sarah spoke up, almost breathless with tension. "He could have crossed into Ojinaga by now." She took a piece of paper out of her pocket and handed it to me. "The license number of his pickup. I wrote it down as he drove off. You call. You tell the sheriff for us, please."

"Where's your telephone?"

Five arms pointed to a small table in the adjacent hall.

I did as Sarah asked, knowing it was probably too late for the sheriff to stop Rano Johnson this side of the border, even if he called the Customs station or Border Patrol for help.

Sheriff Tate's response was brief, and anything but cordial. "Trouble seems to meet you wherever you are. Stay put, Mrs. Jones. I'll want to talk to you as well as the Spiveys." He hung up.

"The sheriff will be here as soon as he can," I told the sisters.

They all looked at Leila, waiting for her to say something. She spoke one terse sentence. "He's wasting his time."

"I'll wait in the pickup," I said. I had the feeling they had things to say to each other that were none of my business. I sat for twenty-six minutes until Skeeter Tate arrived.

"Mrs. Jones, do you ever stay home? What do you know about what happened here today?" he asked.

"Nothing more than what I told you on the telephone. I got here after it was all over."

I followed him into the hacienda. Leila and Hattie did the talking, and in the space of a few words, I understood why. The sisters had used the time I'd been gone to rearrange their story. I wondered what Leila had told the others in order to get them to agree to lying. They looked Tate in the eye, said the deputy had stopped to ask some questions about ranch security in light of all the recent thefts.

Hattie said, "Known him almost all his life—"

"—he worked for us in the summers," Leila said.

Hattie said, "He borrowed some money for something needed for his children—"

"—and for some reason Texana misunderstood and before we could stop her—"

"I see." Tate's tone hit me like cold water. I tried to catch Clara's eye, but she was inspecting the rug.

"Ladies, I'll be going now. Mrs. Jones, may we talk outside?" He went to the door and I followed.

Tate opened his car door, then stopped to look at me, saying, "I had a talk with Crosswell's wife. She confirmed what you told me. I confronted Rano with the photograph of the two of them. I don't see why you have it in for this man, but my suggestion to you is that you drop this now, before Johnson files a libel action against you."

"Meet me at the bottom of the road and we'll talk." I got into my pickup and drove off, leaving the sheriff behind.

I waited at the end of the Spivey road. The sheriff didn't take long to join me. He pushed his hat back on his head, crossed his arms, and leaned against the door of his car, his expression attentive but cautious.

"The sisters are lying and the reason goes back to when Julian Row came to town," I said. "Leila saw Row as a predator stalking her sister. Ella wanted marriage and a life outside the family. Leila thought Ella was making a fool of herself, so she hired the detective that Rano Johnson recommended to her to dig into Row's past. After she found out the kind of man Julian Row was, she may have showed Ella the report, but knowing both of them, I doubt it. I don't think Ella would have believed it. I think Leila came up with a plan to scare Row. I think she had Rano Johnson search Row's room at the Paisano. I drove through town during the blackout and spoke to someone outside the hotel, a man whose voice I couldn't identify at the time because I hadn't ever talked to your deputy. I'm pretty close to certain it was Rano."

Tate said, "What about—"

"Hear me out, then you can tear into my theory. Row must have been sweating underneath all those new western duds he bought, when he found out he'd come to Marfa only to run into the husband and father of the family he'd killed. Why didn't he leave town? Because he must have corralled Ella already. At his age, this was his last hooray or he'd have left town the first time he heard the name Crosswell."

"But—"

"Just a bit more patience. The next part isn't guesswork. Leila admitted to me that she tried to make Row look like a drunken fool in front of Ella by putting peyote in his drink the night of the Marfa Lights Festival. The cactus is growing in a pot on the kitchen windowsill. That went wrong when Clay got the spiked drink and had a really bad reaction."

"So that's what happened."

"Yes. It scared Leila—not because she was worried about Clay, but because she didn't want questions asked. The interesting thing is why, if Leila knew all about Row's past, didn't she just confront him? Because it could have failed. Ella might have simply gone off with Row, to live on her money. Confrontation was out. Leila knew Row might be playing a strong hand. My sister-in-law, Fran, saw Ella and him together at the airport the day she arrived here. Later that night we ran into them dancing on the road, champagne and music and all. Those two were celebrating a marriage. I called the airport. A few days before, Row had chartered a plane for Las Vegas. If Leila knew, she must have wondered if Ella intended to come back. I imagine the bride wanted to keep the marriage secret until she told her sisters. After they announced their happy news to the whole family, my guess is that Leila and Hattie together convinced Ella to hold off on a public announcement in the *Sentinel* until the quarantine was lifted from the cattle and the sisters could celebrate with a party at the ranch. I'll bet even Row fell for that line of reasoning. In Leila, he'd met his equal for strategy. That's when Leila's planning turned deadly. She's on the Marfa gossip grapevine, just like I'm on Polvo's. That's how she learned about Rano Johnson's long-standing infatuation with Howie's wife. Leila had two things Cosmé wanted more than anything in the world: land and money. I think either she offered Johnson both to kill Julian Row or Johnson approached her with the idea. Cosmé knew all about her husband's past. I'll bet she told her lover Howie's whole story more than once in that Ojinaga hotel room."

"You see Miss Leila as some kind of Machiavelli," Tate said drily.

I understood the reference, but I ignored it. "I see her as a old lady who's always gotten her way and can't change now, no matter what it takes. Leila's cold-blooded. She showed her true colors by asking me to warn Howie about the damning facts about him in the detective agency's background check on Row. She told me she wanted to help Howie, but if I'd done as she asked and he'd run, everybody would have believed he did it. I think that's exactly what Leila hoped would happen."

Tate said, "Crosswell didn't bother to run because he was past caring. Here's a man who's been quietly trying to drink himself to death for several years. I think Howie Crosswell killed Row, then decided to let the state of Texas kill him. Finish saying your piece."

"That's it. Rano Johnson pulled the trigger, but Leila Spivey is as much a killer as he is."

"Ever think maybe she kept it more simple?" Tate said. "Told Crosswell who Row was, and then sat back and waited?"

"Maybe she did, and Howie was too far gone in his

alcoholism to act. Tell me this: why did Johnson come to Leila for money? He didn't rob her. It was black-mail."

"You're the only one saying it. It's six of their version, one of yours. You have a fine imagination, Mrs. Jones, but always remember the saying, if it quacks like a duck and walks like a duck, it's likely to be a duck. I've got my ducks all in a row. How about you?" Tate started a chuckle that turned into full-fledged laughter as he got behind the wheel and drove away.

I sat feeling like the fool I'd made of myself, then drove home, where I hit the door talking, my words aimed at the back of Clay's head as he sat at the kitchen table spooning peanut butter out of a jar. ". . . and he's run to Mexico," I was saying as Clay was spreading peanut butter on a cracker.

"What are you doing?" I said, turning over the blue lid of the peanut butter jar on the table in front of him so he could see the white label running across the top marked MOUSE BAIT in black ink.

He sputtered into a napkin. "I ate that stuff," he said.

"It's all right. It's very old peanut butter, that's all. I don't dip the traps in it. I scoop some out and then use a Q-Tip to bait the spring. I'll get the good jar out."

"I don't think I want any more."

"How about a toasted cheese sandwich?"

"Great. I'll get Charlie. He hasn't eaten either." Clay went through and came back with Charlie. I got the pan and the makings of six sandwiches, using butter on the toast so we each needed two napkins to catch the dripping grease. While I worked, I told him what had happened at the ranch.

"How did you find the Spiveys?" Clay asked.

"That's quite a story," I told him.

Long after the food, we were still talking.

"I think I wasted my time giving the sheriff that photograph," I said. "After the job the Spiveys did on me, he won't believe anything I have to say, ever."

"If Rano killed Row he's gotten away with it," Clay said.

"The sheriff still believes Howie Crosswell did it."

"Maybe," Charlie said, "but when he realizes that Rano is gone, he may decide differently. Rano must have been scared. Once the door opened on Johnson's connection with Cosmé there was no end to where the investigation might go. The sheriff will find something, wait and see."

Clay said, "Johnson will vanish in Mexico."

"I wonder if Cosmé will join him," I said.

TWENTY

On Wednesday, the grand jury indicted Howie Crosswell in the murder of Julian Row and we picked up Jake Dare at the airport in Alpine.

On Friday, when we met Fran and Jake for dinner at Picasso's restaurant, it was clear that Jake had moved into defense mode, playing the game by dressing like a down-home man of the West. In Jake's case, this meant gabardine trousers and a suede vest over a blue shirt, his black leather coat flung casually over his arm. Put a Stetson on the man and he could play the Gary Cooper part in a remake of *High Noon*.

Between them, they wore the whole steer. Fran had a fringed jacket over a black leather shirt and pants.

Picasso had reserved a table near the front window

of the Nuevo Eatery, with the owner himself gracing our table. The gentle hum of conversation around us matched the glances in our direction as Marfa made note of Jake's arrival and took a reading on the out-of-town lawyer. Jake might have done away with the three-piece suit but the persona that accompanied it was on full display. He told amusing stories, charmed the restaurant staff, joked and laughed and behaved as if he'd always been a part of Marfa.

With the sheriff, the district attorney, and the county judge primed not to be shown up by the high-powered Houston lawyer, Jake had hit the town aiming to charm. Through friends in common whose names served as introductions, he had met most of the people in town whose good opinion could help with public opinion. As he put it, he wasn't just playing to a jury, but the whole community. It didn't hurt, he said that he felt at home because his wife had just become a property owner and his brother-in-law was the county veterinarian. My trading post got lost somewhere.

"He's already planning his closing argument," Fran said.

"My wife exaggerates," Jake said, forking a bite of the mushroom-stuffed pizza, which Picasso had explained was a specialty of northern Italy. "What's the local feeling about the crime?" He addressed us all with his glance around the table.

"Half and half," Picasso said. "Half the town doesn't think he belongs in jail at all, because of what Row did to his family. The other half is afraid of looking bad by letting a murderer get away, in spite of sympathizing with him."

"We can reassure them on that. Minds are made to be changed," Jake said. "For instance, this deputy Crosswell's wife was involved with. I've put one of my people on him. The fact of the affair will make a nice diversion for the jury, plus create doubt of my client's guilt when I speculate that the deputy could have shot Row knowing the blame would fall on his rival."

When I asked about proof, Jake said, "A good defense lawyer doesn't need proof. Innuendo will do. The courts don't define *reasonable* for jurors." Jake laughed. "It's the doubt planted in their minds that does the trick."

Fran turned the conversation to the gallery, discussing what she called a select list of artists, both local and from Houston, who had agreed to display at the opening, planned for early spring. That and local topics kept the conversation going through dessert, a custard topped with shaved chocolate and spun sugar. After dinner, we parted. Rather then stay at the Paisano, Jake had arranged for private accommodation for himself and his staff in the Highland Street guest house of a local rancher.

Clay drove and I spent the long journey home in thought. Around us, the benign darkness under the starry sky expanded time by its shadowy suggestion of a timeless and limitless horizon. Like Fran, many people found peace here, away from the dangerous shadows of the cities, but as newcomers arrived they chipped away at the open space and disrupted the quiet they came to find. The process saddened me because it was inexorable. Someday this last enchanted landscape would be paved and subdivided, a copy of life elsewhere.

"The news media are going to flock here for this trial," Clay said in a gloomy voice. "Jake's hired a public relations consultant to line up a couple of news magazine television shows and court the Associated Press and Texas media."

"Good thing Jake is photogenic. I guess he'll get Howie a haircut and an agent. What a life. Your love and loss exploited for public consumption."

At the trading post, Charlie had waited up. Clay had an emergency call, a horse down. He changed clothes and took Charlie with him as an extra pair of hands.

I knew better than to wait up. I cleaned Phobe's dirty food dish, changed her water, brushed her, and left her asleep on the bed. I went in front to clear the cash from the register and found on the wooden counter a handwritten notice, probably left by Claudia, announcing that a special Mass to be followed by a barbecue would be held on the following Saturday. I took some tape and went down the aisle, my town shoes making hollow sounds on the wood floor. I pressed the notice against the window and taped it neatly to the glass face-out. That's how invitations are issued around here. We post signs at the two places everyone gets to sooner or later, the trading post and the post office. Everyone is invited and almost everyone shows up for birthdays, weddings, holiday parties. We love any excuse for a fiesta.

Outside the moon had begun to rise, fat and golden, half hidden by a trailing cloud shaded blue. I pulled my jacket tight around me, cut off the lights inside and out, and stepped onto the porch. As an only child, even in close-knit Polvo, I had spent much time in lone adventures and had never been afraid, either of the dark or the loneliness.

The desert in its many forms and patterns was at all times for me a place of refuge. At night the contours that by day were subtle jumped into relief from the starlight. Vega shone bright enough to stand out distinctly from millions of stars that sprinkled the heavens and Venus rose with the moon. Here and there where it pooled, the water of the river glinted like the flaked silver backing of an antique mirror in contrast to the unnatural darkness of the burned-out banks and jagged tree stumps on either side. As I watched the ribbon of road, something long and hunched ran across and vanished against the backdrop of the darker soil. It might have been a small coyote heading to the river for water. Further on, another shadow caught my eye, moving away from the river—a mule deer perhaps, spooked out of hiding by the coyote. The shape shifted as it moved steadily in a line for the trading post. I kept still and watched, hoping it would come close. As it reached the road, it was so well defined in outline that I could identify it, but it wasn't a deer. I watched the measured step. Above, the trailing cloud cleared the moon. Now the phantom could see me standing on the edge of the steps as clearly as I saw it. If *Nuestra Señora* had stepped down from the trading post wall as an apparition and called my name, I couldn't have been more shocked.

Gregorio Esparza called to me, "Have no fear, señora."

The Ojinaga policeman, in baseball cap, cowboy shirt, jeans, and boots, approached. In eloquent Spanish, standing with one foot on the bottom step, he explained he had come on behalf of a mutual friend who wished to speak privately with me on his own behalf. He, Gregorio, personally vouched for his friend's good will toward me and would be grateful if I would listen to his friend's story. Most important, I must, under no circumstances, call the Presidio authorities. He, Gregorio, would be very distressed should I attempt such a thing because he esteemed our mutual trust.

I agreed because, however polite the form, I got the message. I had no choice. I didn't understand what was going on, but I didn't like how it was starting.

"Could we speak outside, here on the porch?" I asked. Gregorio motioned to the darkness and said, "That would suit my friend well."

Another shadow moved forward and Rano Johnson materialized under the light of the moon and moved to the bottom of the steps.

I must have made some inadvertent sound, because Gregorio hastened to "reassure" me with a firm hand on my wrist. "He wants only to speak privately with you. We have been watching for an opportunity." He released my wrist and moved away, saying to Johnson as he passed that he would wait with the truck on the other side.

"You look fit and well for a man in police custody," I said sarcastically. "I'm going to sit down," I added, doing so to cover my fear with action.

"I'll join you," he said, pulling one of the Corona Beer chairs away from mine and into the shadows, so that all I could see of him was the dark gleam of his eyes.

"I'll get right down to it," Johnson said. "I need some help and you're the only person I can ask, first off, because you know what's happened. Some of it anyway. Everybody around here says you're honest. I hear that some people might try to pin the Row murder on me, and I can't let that happen. I want your help clearing my name."

Word passes, I reflected. And too damn fast. I'd put myself in this position by showing the sheriff the photograph Barrilito had taken.

Rather than squirm, I asked questions. "Why did Leila help you? Give you money? Did you threaten her?"

"I asked nicely."

He seemed to be waiting for some comment, so I made a noncommittal sound, something like "Umph."

"I'd better explain," Johnson said. "The old lady hired me to kill Julian Row for her—"

In trying to get up I moved too fast, and my chair

tilted backward, taking me with it. Johnson jumped to his feet and grabbed with both hands, righting me and the chair, saying, "Easy. I'm no killer."

"Oh, that's a comfort," I snapped. That I'd been right about Leila's involvement didn't give me much satisfaction with her accomplice sitting on my front porch. Johnson remained on his feet; I stayed welded to my chair.

He said, "I'd have been a fool to take a risk like that, but the cash offer was very nice. She suggested I use it to sweeten Cosmé, so I told the old lady, sure, I'd do it, but she'd have to pay half up front." He laughed, still pleased at his own trick. "What could she do when I didn't kill him, take me to court for breach of contract? When he was found shot, I figured somebody had made me some easy money."

"Why did you run?"

"Tate had been acting suspicious of me, suggesting I might volunteer to take a polygraph to clear things up, saying how it didn't look good for me to be investigating Howie if there was a conflict of interest." Johnson yanked his chair over to mine and straddled it. "I knew if old Skeeter started digging in earnest, he'd find out things, like how I'd been supplementing my income, so I figured it was Mexico or jail. I stopped on the way to get the rest of money and the old lady balked, so I had to explain that she could go down for solicitation of murder on my testimony. After that she got nicer."

"But, if you didn't kill Row," I said, "are you saying Howie did?"

"I don't know who killed Row. That's what I want you to help me find out."

Johnson scared me half to death when he reached into a pocket of his coat.

"Easy," he said, "it's not a gun. It's information I got on Row from that PI agency. I called them up and told them how I was working for Leila Spivey. Well, in a way, I was, wasn't I," he joked. "They didn't know I wasn't still a law officer in good standing. This is a list of Row's ex-wives, the ones he swindled, and the relatives of Howie's dead wife. Five names. They're who I'd start with if I was investigating the murder. One of them must know something. They each had reason to hate him. Start with the wife's family first."

"Start what? What am I supposed to do?"

"I ran the names through the Department of Motor Vehicles to get addresses. Telephone them, talk to them, see what you can find out."

Johnson shoved the list into my hands, got to his feet, and said, "If you need to get in touch, Gregorio says you have his number."

"Wait here a minute," I told him, getting up and moving to the door. I didn't need to turn on the light to find my way to the register. I'd grown up playing jacks and hide-and-seek with my friends in the trading post. I put my hand on the badge, and walked back to give it to Johnson.

"This is yours," I said, holding it out to him. "It

was finding it that first made me wonder about you—whether or not you might have been Barrilito's connection, the person he planned to snitch to, and if for some reason you'd failed him."

Johnson flared with ready anger. "Failed him, hell. That sawed-off stump of a Barrilito threatened to expose me. He expected me to pay him off." He stretched out his hand for the badge, and I moved back, appalled by his cold attitude toward Barrilito. He might not, as he claimed, be a killer, but he had a killer's heart. I let go of the badge and it hit the porch boards with a clunk and lay between us.

"Hey, how many times do I have to tell you? I'm no killer," Johnson said defensively.

"Tell me how you supplemented your income."

"I started out with small things, equipment thefts, stuff like that. Pretty soon I was approached. Now I work with the powers that be. I don't see the drug suppliers as any different from any other businessmen with a product to sell that people are clamoring for. What I do for money is no more than lots of *fronterizos* do."

"And lots don't."

"That's not the point," he said explosively. "Look, I admit I told my bosses about Barrilito. I had to. They don't tolerate any kind of interference."

"Then you as good as killed him," I said accusingly.

"He was just a street vendor," Johnson said impatiently, trying to justify himself. "Nobody cares that he's dead. A year from now, nobody will remember a street vendor killed in a forgotten border town."

I thought of Pachá, of Barrilito's sons. They would remember. I would remember.

I said, "His family—"

"Is well taken care of. His sons have gone to work for my friends. The offer of employment was made just in case, you understand, they found anything that might expose me or endanger my friends. Making good money is better than being dead, don't you think? Too bad their old man didn't show as much sense. If he'd asked for a job instead of making threats, he'd be alive today. Threats are never tolerated. You'd do well to remember that, living right on the border like you do."

"Is *that* a threat?" I said, my own strain showing itself in anger.

He stretched out a hand in a gesture of supplication and said, his voice pleading, "Just help me keep my name out of the Row killing. For my kids, please. Row's trial is going to make headlines. This high-priced killer-lawyer of old Howie's will see to that. There won't be any place my family can move that somebody won't remember the Row murder. I don't want my kids to live with that the rest of their lives."

He turned to go. "Gregorio is going to be tired of waiting for me. You do like I said. Check out those relatives."

TWENTY-ONE

For once, I couldn't operate on border time. Speed, perhaps downright haste, seemed desirable. I made the first call to directory assistance the next morning and got the number for the first name on Rano Johnson's list, an F. T. McMurtry in Grandtree, Texas. The female voice that answered spoke slowly and sounded either old or ill, or both. I identified myself and asked to speak to Mr. McMurtry.

I heard a clank as the woman put down the receiver. "Frank, Frank, Frank," she shouted, her voice panicky.

Footsteps and another female voice came faintly over the line, saying soothingly, "Hush, love. Everything is fine. Here, sip your juice." The same voice, the tone normal and firm, said, "Hello. Who is this?" into my ear.

I identified myself a second time and again asked for Mr. McMurtry.

"He'd dead," the woman told me. "He's been dead these past four years. Heart attack."

"I'm sorry. Are you Mrs. McMurtry?" I asked.

"Mrs. McMurtry is my mother. That was her who answered the telephone. She's got early onset Alzheimer's."

"I'm sorry." Lonely, I thought, wanting to share the problem, even with a stranger on the telephone. "Then Megan was your sister? I'm calling about her death."

"Wait and let me get on the extension."

She picked up again. "Megan was my baby sister. I don't dare say her name in front of mother. It upsets her and gets her to asking why Megan hasn't visited her, just like she called now for Frank, my dad. Thinks they're both still alive. We thought Mother would be the one to grieve herself to death over Megan dying like that, but it was Dad. Why are you asking about Megan?"

I had decided on a response, a lie, to questions like that before I called. "I'm really interested in trying to locate relatives of hers who might be interested in Howie Crosswell's welfare. He has been arrested for the murder of Julian Row, the man responsible for Megan's death."

"Row's dead? Well, I won't pretend I'm sorry. Now Howie I am sorry about, but who could blame him?

Of course, he moved straight out of our lives after the funeral. It was like we reminded him of Megan and he couldn't bear it. That, and him and my brother had words. John blamed Howie for not being home to take care of Megan and the babies. You can't reason with grief. Them dying like that tore us all up, real bad. We all loved her. She was that kind of person, and being the baby of the family, too, it was hard." She muffled the telephone and called out, "I'm coming, Mother. I'm right here." And in my ear, "I've got to go now. You might try my brother John in Castroville—I'm coming, Mother." She hung up before I could ask for a number.

I rechecked Rano Johnson's list. No John McMurtry listed. Where was Castroville? If it was in Texas, I'd never heard of it. If it wasn't, I'd have to call the McMurtry house again. I went to look at the wall map and found Castroville marked as a small circle thirty miles west of San Antonio. Directory assistance had a number for a John McMurtry. I rang, an answering machine picked up, and I left my name, number, and message after the beep as instructed by a male voice that sounded very Texan, like a thousand others I'd heard in a lifetime.

Between customers, I made directory assistance calls for listings in the cities where Julian Row's ex-wives had last lived, with only one success. I presumed the other two had either moved, remarried, or both. The one I located shouted "wahoo!" when I told her Row had been murdered, then bent my ear for over an hour with every detail of Row's courtship, their marriage, and their divorce, including the amount of her lawyer's fees. She was bitter, angry, hurt, and resentful, and said if I gave her the name of a bank in Marfa she'd send a check in Howie's name for "killing that no-good bastard for me." I decided anyone that candid, had she killed Row, would have waited for the sheriff with the smoking gun in hand.

Clay didn't make it home for lunch, and Charlie had gone on his calls with him, so I snacked and tried the Castroville number again. Still the answering machine. I left a message with my name and number saying his sister had told me to call regarding Megan McMurtry Crosswell's death. I located my copy of the *Texas Guidebook* and read about the place.

Most of the homes in the town were on the National Register of Historic Places. It sounded enchanting, a village built by European settlers from the Alsace region. The small houses, according to the guidebook, would have looked at home on the Rhine River.

I waited until the evening, tried John McMurtry's number again. No luck. Rano Johnson's list had accomplished nothing except to run up my telephone bill. I'd give this McMurtry man one more call in a couple of days.

I was guilt-driven. Thanks to my interference and Barrilito's photograph, I had unintentionally strengthened the case against Howie, and simultaneously given Jake Dare his best hope of putting the murder on Rano.

Thoroughly depressed, I went to cook a pot of stew for Clay and Charlie, so it could be warmed over if they were late. As I peeled potatoes and carrots, I thought about how many people Julian Row's careless, casual greed had harmed. His ex-wives, Megan Crosswell and her children, of course, but also Frank McMurtry, dead of grief and shock, his only surviving daughter left to care for her mother alone. And what of Megan's brother? Had he gotten over the bitterness his sister spoke of, or did he carry it like a weight? The injury Row had done to Howie might as well have been death, might still be if he were convicted, though Jake wouldn't like to hear me use that word.

TWENTY-TWO

Claudia had misplaced the banner and Charlie and Ruben searched for it while Clay and I set up the tables on the swept grounds in front of the church, while three of the high school kids inflated balloons and tied them in bunches for Señor Luna to staple to each table as a centerpiece.

Our fiestas are fulsome events, overflowing with abundant food, goodwill, and energy. The ladies of Polvo had prepared gallons of iced tea. Barrels of chipped ice held chilled cans of Dr Pepper, Coke, Pepsi, Sidral Mundet, a favorite Mexican soft drink, and Topo-Chico mineral water. Foil-wrapped desserts, salads, and salsas waited in cars and pickups for the tables to be readied. The pungent, smokey smell of barbecued *cabrito* overwhelmed the scent of incense inside the church, where the doors stood open, waiting for the guests of honor, the thirty marines and three civilians who'd saved Polvo and the trading post. Color was everywhere: in the garlands of paper greenery and bright flowers decorating the church doors and the ends of the pews; in the jewel-like votive candles burning beneath the statue of Our Lady of Guadalupe; in the starched and ironed gloss of the Sunday-best clothes.

With only ten minutes to spare before Mass, Charlie showed up holding a folded white banner, held it up to Ruben, who climbed the ladder, and tied the left-hand corner in place, then moved across to fix the other side. Just as Ruben and Charlie removed the ladder, the marines strolled up, neat in pressed camouflage, caps, and boots, smiling self-consciously as all of Polvo clapped and stood back to let our guests enter the church first beneath the banner that read MIL GRACIAS MARINES & BOOTS, JOE, BARRY.

Daniel Ramos waved his camera and asked the guests to line up in front of the church for a group picture. Putting the civilians in front, the marines organized themselves in neat rows behind the two men. "Boots," my blond rescuer from the day of the fire, was absent. When everyone was ready, Daniel called out, "Show me some teeth!" Someone else shouted, "Say Tripoli," the marines smiled, and Daniel snapped a series of photographs.

The church bell tolled, Father Jack came to the

doors robed in green and yellow and ready to pat each guest on the back as they walked inside and filled the front pews reserved for them, while three guitar players strummed the *Marine Hymn*. The priest sailed through Mass in twenty minutes, replaced his homily with a brief but eloquent tribute to our guests, and after he blessed us, we stormed out the doors to begin a vigorous assault on the food.

Fiesta means eating, music, dancing, and talking, all going on simultaneously. Clay and I wandered around, visiting here and there with friends and neighbors, chatting with marines nervously tasting the *cabrito*. We ate the tender meat rolled in flour tortillas and tempted the guests to try the various fresh salsas.

The day wore on under the immense sky, mellow and warm. The marines relaxed and enjoyed themselves. More cameras and even a few camcorders came out and soon everyone was posing, smiling, and laughing. Joe, the other bulldozer operator who saved the trading post, came over to me and asked would I mind if we could find someone to take our picture together. Father Jack heard and took Joe's camera. We posed smiling into the lens.

"I'm sorry Boots missed the group picture," I said to Joe after Father Jack had handed back the camera and gone on his way. "We consider both of you real VIPs."

"I thought he'd be here by now," Joe said.

"Tell him I asked about him. I intend to put both of you on my Christmas list."

"Glad to have helped," he said earnestly. He searched in his pockets. "I've got a card here somewhere . . . here you go. The boss's business address."

As I tucked the card into my pocket, a pretty young Polvo girl tapped Joe on the shoulder and asked him to dance. I excused myself and looked around for Clay. I was tired and ready to go home.

Father Jack's voice boomed out from the steps of the church. When he wanted to be heard, he didn't need a bull horn. "Okay folks, gather 'round. We've added a little extra flair to this fiesta and come up with some contests and prizes for the winners. It's time for our border games, honoring those who cross and those who catch 'em, sometimes." That got a big laugh. "No skill involved, just speed and gluttony. The El Paso climb is first. Participants are timed from a five-yard starting point until both feet touch the ground on the other side of the ten-foot-high chain-link fence section, supplied by Garza Fencing in Presidio. No wire cutters allowed. The winner gets the section of fence. Next is the checkpoint sprint, pitting all comers against our three fleet-footed Border Patrol agents. The winner gets a T-shirt that says FASTEST FEET ON THE BORDER."

"Not fair, Padre," someone shouted. "Make those agents run with sidearms, cuffs, and cartridge belts!" Father Jack waited for the laughter to die before continuing.

"And my personal favorite, the tortilla-eating contest. We encourage our marine friends especially to enter this one. The winner gets a bottle of antacid tablets supplied by Texana's Trading Post. Judges and contestants, take your places. Let the games begin."

I located Clay, only to have him tell me Father Jack had asked him to help judge the tortilla-eating contest. "I couldn't turn him down," Clay said. "Not after chewing him out over the shrine business."

"Guilt is highly motivational. I guess it's better than if he'd asked you to be a contestant. You won't be bilious all night. Is Charlie staying?"

"He is a contestant."

"I should have known."

"You're going home, then?"

"Right now. I think I need to check on the pilgrims. I feel better when I'm there to keep an eye on things," I said.

I worked my way to the pickup, pleased to find we'd been right to leave it far enough along the road not to get blocked in. I was home in five minutes and doing a brisk business in canned meats, matches, baby food, diapers, bottled water, paper towels, travel pillows, which they used for kneelers, charcoal briquets for cooking fires, and the fifty-five-gallon metal drums that are cut in half and used for cookers. I was seriously thinking of making fresh sandwiches to sell. Claudia had been right when she'd said I was blessed by *Nuestra Señora*.

I was so busy, I didn't have time to remove my jacket until the last customer had paid for six votive candles. It was nearly closing time and I reminded her not to leave candles burning after dark. She assured me the candles were for her friend, who was coming to pray *mañana*. As soon as she was out the door, I went to the back, kicked off my shoes, put on the coffee, and tossed my jacket at the coat rack. Phobe came running out from one of her hiding places, wrapped her big paws around my ankle, and nipped me lightly with her teeth to remind me she had been alone most of the day. Then, standing like a gawky adolescent, all legs, feet, and eyes, she watched while I poured a cup of the coffee and put on a video of *Enchanted April*. As soon as I hit the couch, she hit me, landing from her flying leap on my lap and very nearly knocking the breath out of me. She arranged herself with hind legs stretched along the cushions, the rest of her more or less on me, her head resting on my arm. She relaxed instantly, flexing her paws once, enough to remind me I still hadn't told Clay to trim her claws. We remained in companionable comfort through the movie.

By the time the movie ended, I assumed Clay must have had an emergency call. No tortilla-eating contest lasted until dark and after. I heard the front bell ring and said a silent curse for not having locked up after seeing out the last pilgrim. I hustled Phobe aside and got up.

I stepped into the front and into the dark. "I'll have the lights on in a sec," I called. With my left hand I reached for the switch and touched a face. I jumped back but not fast enough. The air moved. The blow hit my cheekbone, the sound of impact a crush of bone that sent shockwaves of pain radiating through my body. I choked on my own cry of anguish and fear as I hit the floor. A massive, dark shape bore down on me, straddling my hips with such weight that it felt like a horse had rolled over on me. "I got your messages," a cold, male voice said as something hard pressed against my throat. I gagged, grasped it with my hands, fighting desperately to push it away. I felt the rusted iron surface and the S-shaped ending of the old branding iron from the display behind the counter. I couldn't shift it. I kicked, my feet flaying the air uselessly. I raised my arms, trying to get my fingers to his eyes, but his hold outreached my grasp and I barely touched the line of his jaw.

I clawed for air, my head exploding with pressure that boomed in my ears like a kettledrum. I heard a scream of pain and thought it must be me. I could no longer feel the weight on my throat and thought I must be dead, but the screaming went on and on. Tears rolled down the sides of my face and ran into my ears. Hungry for air, I breathed open-mouthed and gasping. I rolled over and pawed the air, trying to find the counter to pull myself up, knowing without thought that if I wasn't dead then I would be if I let myself lose consciousness. I found the wall instead and leaned my weight against it as I pushed myself upward toward the light switch. When the lights came on, I saw my attacker writhing with Phobe on his back, the claws of one paw embedded in one side of his neck, the other paw tearing into the flesh of his face, her jaws clamped around the back of his neck as if he were a deer she was trying to bring down. Blood splattered in thick drops as he spun around trying to sling her off. The harder he struggled the tighter she held and the harder she bit.

"Get it off," he screamed. "Get it off!"

In an adrenaline high that restored my thinking with a sudden spurt of oxygenated blood to my brain, I grabbed my pistol from the shelf beneath the counter. If I could manage to get Phobe off of him, I intended to protect us, Phobe and myself, and shoot if I had to.

If I could get her to release her prey. I'd once tried to remove a dead jackrabbit from the kitchen table where Phobe had started to consume it. She'd flattened her ears, narrowed her eyes, growled, and raised a wide paw to swat the metal dustpan out of my hand with enough force to send it flying against the wall with a bang. Clay had said that I could hardly blame her for protecting her kill.

"Keep still," I said, approaching the pair slowly, "and keep quiet. You're making it worse by fighting her."

To my shock, with what must have been incredible willpower, he obeyed, lowering his arms and dropping, first to his knees, then to all fours. Blood dripped onto the floorboards beneath him.

I called Phobe's name, made soothing sounds, and reached out a hand where she could first see it before touching the back of her head ever so slightly. She growled and tried to make a shaking motion with her head as she tightened her jaws. The man made a moaning sound and I saw him quake.

I knelt beside them and placed my hand on Phobe's back, feeling her skin flinch with tension. I talked to her, rubbed her, then slipped the gun into my pocket to use both hands. With one on her neck, I put the other in front of her nose so she could smell me, talking all the while. She rolled her eyes toward me, then unclamped her jaws to sniff my fingers. Knowing she could take my fingers off, I put my hand on her paw where it clung to the man's face. "This will hurt," I said. I extricated her foot one toe at a time, then pulled it away. He sagged and went flat to the floor. Phobe made a throaty growl. Raising her head, she looked into my eyes and bent her head to my hand to lick me, leaving my fingers streaked with blood. I lifted her in my arms, felt her tension. As I carried her to the laundry room, she panted open-mouthed. She had exhausted herself. I put her down on her bed. She needed me to stay with her, but I couldn't. I wanted to collapse beside her, but I couldn't. I had things to do and I was at the end of my strength. As I closed the door behind me with one hand, I took the gun out of my pocket with the other. I looked down at the cheap revolver I'd bought two years ago and hoped it wouldn't fail me if I needed it. I flipped open the cylinder to make sure it had a bullets in all six chambers, but I couldn't seem to focus clearly. I touched my left cheek near my eye. The hard lump felt like the size of a baseball and my eye was swollen shut. I made do with feeling for the .38-caliber cartridges. I walked slowly through out private quarters, more than half expecting my attacker to jump me on the way. At the door to the front, I peeked around, saw a foot and part of his leg still on the floor. He hadn't moved. I stopped biting my lip.

Arms and legs sprawled, the side of his face that I could see looked strangely gaunt and pale, the color of watery pie dough from loss of the blood that darkened the floor in a widening arc, like a profane halo around his head. I would have thought him dead, but for the scrambling movement his fingers made in response to the sound of my shocked cry, uttered involuntarily at the sight of his clawed face and in recognition of who my attacker was.

"I'll get help, Boots," I said, pivoting and running for the telephone. "Polvo, the trading post. Help. We need help," I heard myself say frantically, some part of me knowing that I was near the end not only of physical strength but wits. I rallied myself to coherence long enough to say that a man was bleeding badly and needed a helicopter. I dropped the telephone, desperately trying to think ahead. Towels. I need towels. I yanked them from the bathroom shelves and carried them bunched in my arms back to the front. Putting them beyond the blood but within reach, I grasped his shoulders, just managing to tug and pull until I got him over on his back. I lifted his shoulders across my lap and cradled his head, cushioning it with jeans I pulled down around us from a table. I folded a towel and pressed it tightly against the torn artery in his neck. His one good eye stared up into mine. The other was ruined, ripped by Phobe's claws. I tried to comfort him. "You'll be okay," I said, hoping it wasn't a lie.

His eye fluttered, focused. He raised his hand and grasped my arm. "I killed Row. I put the gun in Howie's studio. Tell them." His hand dropped and he closed his eye. Minute by minute, it seemed, I replaced a sodden towel with a clean one. Nothing stopped the blood that flowed from his neck in spurts with each beat of his heart. As we sat seeped in the wet of blood, suffocated by the smell of blood, I clutched him and prayed an undistinguished prayer of mindless need and fear.

I heard footsteps. Someone entered from behind. My hand found the gun where I'd placed it on the floor, I thumbed the hammer back, and raised it in a shaking hand, turning my head, trying to get full peripheral vision with one eye.

"Texana, hon!"

It was Clay. I lowered the gun and said, "I'm fine. I've called for help."

I sensed him kneel beside me on my blind side. His hand touched my shoulder and rested there. After some moments, he spoke. "Let me help you up. I'll take over with him."

I looked around. "I'm out of towels."

Clay touched his fingers to Boots's neck, then rolled back his eyelid. He pressed his hand over mine and said, "He doesn't need a towel now."

He lifted Boots's shoulders and moved him off my lap, then helped me to get up. "If you can manage it, I think I need to know what happened and where Phobe is," he said, looking back over his shoulder at Boots.

"She is safe in the laundry room. He tried to kill me, strangle me. Phobe jumped him."

"Let's get you on the couch where I can look at that eye."

"Is it going to be black?"

"Hon, the whole side of your face is going to be black," he said, hauling me to my feet and propelling me forward.

He seemed relieved when I told him that I'd been able to see out of that eye before the swelling got so bad. He brought me pillows and covered me with a blanket, gave me three ibuprofen, put a cold compress for wrapping horses' legs around my neck, handed me a smaller one for my cheek and eye, and tucked a hot water bottle under my feet.

"See to Phobe," I told him. "She was so scared." I closed my eyes and slept.

Later, I heard voices but couldn't distinguish the words. More voices and footsteps on the wooden floor.

"Can you talk to the sheriff, hon, before they airlift you to the hospital?"

I threw back the blanket and raised myself to a sitting position. Skeeter Tate pulled a chair over and sat down facing me, hunched over with his elbows resting on his knees. "What happened here?" he asked.

I asked Clay to hand me my jacket from the coat rack. He thought I was cold and draped it over my shoulders. I pulled it around and felt in the pocket for the business card Joe had given me at the fiesta.

"The man out there, Boots, made—what do you call it—a dying declaration," I said, "that he murdered Julian Row." I handed the card to Tate.

J. M. Construction

John "Boots" McMurtry—Owner
401 Marquis St.
Castroville, Texas

"This tells me nothing, I know who John McMurtry was, the civilian contractor handling some of the road work. It doesn't tell me why he would have murdered Row or why I should believe your statement that he did. A dying declaration has to be made to an officer of the law or court. Anything else is just hearsay and that's not evidence. Got anything else you want to tell me?"

"Howie Crosswell's dead wife, Megan, was Mc-Murtry's younger sister."

I told Tate the gist of my telephone conversation with Boots's sister and about the messages I'd left on John McMurtry's machine.

"Between hitting me and strangling me, Boots said,

'I got your messages.' He must have called and had them played back, jumped to the conclusion that I knew who he was and his connection to Megan. All he had to do was wait until after the pilgrims cleared out, and see which pickups were here. If Clay's was gone and mine was here, he knew he had me alone."

"It was more than that," Clay said. "Just as the fiesta was winding down, I got a message that a man called in to the church to have relayed to me. All the caller said was he needed the vet bad, and drive up Pinto Canyon until I saw a pickup waiting. Charlie went with me. We drove damn near to Highway Ninety. Nothing. Not a pickup on the road."

"You're assuming it was McMurtry getting you out of the way," Tate said. "How many times a year do you get false alarm calls like that?"

"Maybe once in the last five years. You're hunting a cold scent with that idea. Get his phone records. You'll see."

"Sheriff," I said, "talk to—"

"Mrs. Jones," Tate said, "you have a bad habit of telling me how to conduct an investigation. As long as we're playing 'what if,' what if you're into drug smuggling. What if you've been serving as a contact and pickup point for mules moving drugs. What if McMurtry found out, saw something he shouldn't. What if your husband made up that tale about the emergency message. Maybe the two of you made up that whole murder scene out there, set that wild animal of yours onto the man to mark him, then made sure the damage to his neck was bad enough to kill him before—"

Clay was on his feet, restraining himself from grabbing Tate by balling both hands into fists. "I've heard damn well all I want to from you, Tate. We're not murderers. We're not dope dealers. And we aren't listening to any more of your half-baked ideas. Boots just admitted murdering Row. Howie's lawyer and the district attorney can fight it out in court."

Tate stood up. As he marched out, he flung back one last threat at us. "I've a good mind to cage that bobcat and remove her as a public danger."

As the paramedics came in to help me to the helicopter Clay told me not to worry about what Tate said. "The sheriff has a lot more to worry about. I'm the county vet and the one who has the responsibility of determining if an animal is a danger to the community. I can put her under quarantine right here with us."

The paramedics let me get up from the couch and lie down on the stretcher, then strapped me down.

Clay held my hand, talking as I was carried out. "They can't fault Phobe for protecting you. She thinks of us as family, bobkittens, if you will. We'll restrict her to our living quarters to be on the safe side."

I closed my eyes as Clay's hand fell away and the stretcher was lifted into place on the helicopter. I didn't say what I feared. That there were too many people in the world who thought of animals as senseless beings that reacted and acted solely on instinct, without feeling or direction. My own observations had taught me differently, but who would listen?

TWENTY-THREE

A shame we didn't get to trial," Jake said. "We had a Shakespearean tragedy. Young soldier off to war, a beautiful young wife and innocent children slain, a despicably avaricious villain. I would have had the jury in tears with my summation. A trial would have been a boon to the community, too. Rooms and houses rented out to the media, some nice television exposure. Restaurants doing triple the business. Liquor sales quadrupled. It would have put Marfa on the map. Too bad my client's interest had to come first. If I'd been the district attorney, I'd have pressed the case, but then if he'd have been me, he could have won."

Jake shook hands with Clay and me. Fran hugged Clay hard and kissed me lightly. Most of the left side of my face was bandaged to protect my reconstructed cheekbone. The plastic surgeon would remove the stitches in three more days. Fran walked arm-in-arm with her husband to the rented Suburban for the drive to the airport. She was going back to Houston, keeping her house in Marfa as a vacation home.

As Clay had told Sherriff Tate, proving the case against Howie was the district attorney's problem. After a two-hour conversation face-to-face and in private with Jake, the district attorney, a fussy, cautious man, had dropped all charges against Howie Crosswell, issuing a statement that his office had compelling and credible evidence that a man, now dead, had committed the crime for which Mr. Crosswell had been arrested.

TWENTY-FOUR

On a night of no moon, with only the luminous stars for light, Rano Johnson crossed the Rio Grande again and knocked on the back door.

I was washing dishes at the sink in front of the uncurtained kitchen window when I saw a shadowy form against the light-colored gravel spread between the trading post and the clinic. "Someone's out back," I said to Clay.

He went to get his gun, the new one he'd bought after I'd been attacked. The Beretta M9 in hand, he answered the three taps at the door by putting on the outside light. I saw Rano step back into the arc of white so we could see him clearly. Clay looked at me and I nodded an okay.

Clay opened the door. Johnson, his eye on the gun, said, "Can't be too cautious this close to the border." Clay stepped aside and the former-deputy-turned-felon walked in. He had on a blue baseball cap, a black bomber jacket zipped tight against the winter cold, jeans, and boots. Everything about him, from his hair to his ice-blue eyes, looked tired and older.

"I came to thank you," he said.

His eyes rested on my face, uncertain, as he should have been, of his welcome. I had a series of faint scars where the plastic surgeon had done his meticulous work, but the former deputy had no way of knowing that this did not bother me.

I invited Johnson to sit down at the table and we joined him. Clay slipped the gun into his belt.

Johnson kept his hands clenched together on the table. I noticed how his face had grown fresh lines of tension, and I wondered about his life on the other side. When he spoke, his voice was as tight as his clinched hands. "The high sheriff must be disappointed he couldn't nab either me or Howie."

"I don't much like him," I said, "but I think you do him an injustice. He's only just learning the border."

"Yeah, I guess so. Maybe I'm just learning the border myself. I wrote to Cosmé. Asked her to join me. She never answered." He flattened his wide hands against the table and pushed himself to his feet.

I couldn't think of anything to say to him except, "Be careful."

"Too late for that now, but thanks. Mind cutting off that outside light before I step out?" Clay flipped the switch, and Johnson slipped out the door into the dark.

TWENTY-FIVE

Father Jack knelt in the front pew, praying. I lit a candle and added it to those already burning beneath the statue of the Virgin of Guadalupe. The white walls of the church looked as cold as the outside temperature felt, absorbing the warmth of the tiny flames as they flickered. Someone had placed red plastic roses in a turquoise painted flower pot as an offering for the patroness of the Americas, and on a folded paper beneath the homely vessel was a note, no doubt explaining the petitioner's need, in case the Virgin should wish to read it and intercede.

I heard Father Jack's knees crack as he rose. As always, when he smiled on seeing me or any and all of his far-flung parishioners, I wondered where this man and priest got such reserves of goodwill and never-flagging energy that he could respond to our endless demands on his time with such patience.

"You look as if you need to talk," he said.

"Yes, I do."

"We've a better chance of not being disturbed at the house. Come along."

The priest's house once belonged to Polvo's octagenarian fortune teller Doña Aurora. At her death her family gave the small adobe to the church. Her pot plants were gone from the patio and inside, books and papers had replaced the seer's herbs, candles, and saints painted on tin, but the far wall still had row after row of framed pictures of generations of children to whom Doña Aurora had been honorary godmother.

Father Jack moved a stack of books from an armchair and invited me to sit. He lifted a sweater and some shoes from another chair for himself.

"We have all the time in the world," he said, leaning back and resting his hands across his stomach.

"This won't take that long," I told him. He sat as I'd seen him many times, leaning forward, hands folded, index fingers pressed against his lips, compressing them, his eyes neutrally alert.

"Ever since the Crosswell business, it has bothered me that Leila thinks she got away with hiring a murder. I bet she doesn't believe Boots was the killer. Now that Rano's in Mexico she's been heard to say that the sheriff and the DA conspired to cover up for Rano out of embarrassment that a deputy was a crook. It also bothers me that Rano Johnson got away with having Barrilito murdered by his friends."

"Does it surprise you, evil seemingly triumphant? The amoral and immoral always have an edge in this world. They play by no rules save their own."

"So they *win*? Where's the justice in that?"

"I never said they win, but sometimes justice is beyond the obvious, that we can discern anyway. Imagine carrying around the baggage of guilt for the rest of your life."

"I don't notice guilt having that much effect."

"Guilt manifests itself in subtle ways," Father Jack said. "It consumes, like cancer, destroying everything but itself."

Without intending it, I must have let my skepticism show, because the priest sat up and put on his schoolmaster's face.

"Look at the story in Genesis of Cain and Abel," he said. "Abel was living a good life that was pleasing to God, when Cain murdered him. Abel was dead. He certainly didn't get justice, unless you believe that pleasing God is reward in itself, which I do, and if I'm wrong, a greater fool never lived. Cain, on the other hand, got another chance. God banished him from the land he loved and made him a wanderer, but Cain went on to build a city and found a tribe. The mark of Cain wasn't, as so many seem to think, the mark of a murderer. God branded Cain to protect him, so that no man's hand would be raised against him, but Cain had to live to a ripe old age with guilt wrapped around his soul like a slow noose. Guilt which, by his own words, was more than he could bear."

"That's not very satisfactory," I said.

"You think like a theoretical physicist. You want a Theory of Everything, one answer that resolves all your questions. But there are things in this life that human beings aren't meant to understand."

"Could you give a little more than that?"

"All right. As to Leila, she willed murder. That's as damning as committing it. As a priest I have to point out that time is not on her side, and judgment will be done. But if you insist on having justice in this life, for all her overweening pride and frantic efforts to intervene in her sister's life, what has Leila accomplished? She was too late to stop her sister marrying a scoundrel, and the details about Row that she wanted hidden were made public in a big way."

"And Rano?" I said.

"That's an easy one. He lost everything, wife and children, home, lover, and a job that by all accounts he was good at until he let himself be corrupted into crime. He should pray for the mark of Cain to be on him, because he's a walking dead man. What use is he now to his drug smuggling pals? He's not family. He's not a friend. To them he's a gringo-fied Hispanic they'll trust even less than they trust one another. Sooner or later, they'll kill him for what he knows about them." Father Jack settled back in his chair. "Feeling better now?"

"I'll have to think about it," I said, rising to go and

giving him a smile to acknowledge his effort.

"See," he said, "you're smiling. Just the thought of all that earthly retribution bucks you up. You'll have to say ten Hail Marys as penance for taking pleasure in the misery of others."

"I'd think I'll light a candle for Barrilito's soul instead," I said.

TWENTY-SIX

The UPS driver balanced two large boxes in front of him and, on top of those, one thinner cardboard container. I signed the screen on the pad, letting him put the two larger boxes behind the counter to wait for the rancher who had ordered the stereo parts to pick up. The third package had been addressed to me in Fran's rounded handwriting and marked FRAGILE. I cut the outside tape with the blade of my pocket knife. Nesting inside enough bubblewrap to mail twenty packages was a painting done in acrylics and ready to hang in its plainly expensive silver-finished frame. I carried it to the living area, took down the faded print of the Texas hill country that had been my grandmother's, and hung Howie Crosswell's work of art in its place.

He had painted the Marfa Lights, the foreground suggested in shaded colors of the night, deep greens, blackish blues, and rich browns, in which Howie had indicated the rocks and grasses of the Mitchell Flats, dominated by the rising mountains behind. Five mystery lights showed in the middle ground, luminous globes of silver with hints of faint color.

That night, I took Clay for a long drive, starting at sunset. By nine, we had parked in a spot I hadn't visited since high school. I had trusted memory to find the old back gate into the ranch and from there to follow the ruts of the long-disused track that led almost to the base of the mountains. I turned off the lights and we waited, talking quietly in the peaceful dark.

"So this is where you and Andalon used to come when you dated," Clay said.

"We used to drink a beer and discuss the people we dated and talk about our grandiose schemes for the future. We saw the lights maybe three out of the four or five times we came here before graduation. I remember one time—look!

A silver star the size of a baseball flickered and flared at the mountain base, floating upward before blinking out. Instantly, another appeared to the left, pulsating yellow, then separating into two oblongs that shifted apart and moved forward. Another flared and joined the pair, dancing on air in a silent ballet without pattern or rhythm. One skimmed along the ground, growing in size as it came directly toward us.

I heard Clay's intake of breath as it grew larger, the light inside it color shifting, like lights within lights. Its edges grew softer and more diffuse until it enveloped the front end of the pickup in a misty glow of shimmering, blue-white light. My back was pressed tightly against the seat. I counted three seconds until it blinked out.

"I'd forgotten how beautiful they were," I said.

For thirty minutes more, we watched the more distant lights wink on and off without a repeat of the wondrous close-up. As I started the motor, Clay said, "Amazing. Beautiful and amazing. To think people have been seeing these lights for nearly a hundred and fifty years, and yet no one can explain them."

"Father Jack was right," I said.

"About what?"

"That there are some things we aren't meant to understand."

EPILOGUE

Within days after the murder case against him was dismissed, Cosmé and Howie Crosswell appeared as a happy, hand-holding couple on *Inside Edition*. Their new agent parlayed the publicity into a six-figure book deal tentatively titled *Revenge in the High Desert*, and Julian Row's ex-wife, the talkative one who had celebrated Row's death, joined the Crosswells on the talk-show circuit.

Additional success came to Howie when Picasso offered him the use of an empty feed store owned by the Beens family for a studio, paying for the renovation in return for the exclusive rights for the Beens-Dare Gallery to market Howie's Ghost Paintings, as the media had dubbed the portraits of his dead wife and children.

Howie agreed, and Fran opened a second Beens-Dare Gallery in Houston to handle the overflow from the prolific and now famous painter.

At the same time Howie and Cosmé began rebuilding their lives, Father Jack joined Clay and me at a church in Ojinaga to witness the baptism of Pachá's infant daughter, christened Maria Brava Soto. Father Jack had brought along a check for mother and daughter, monies collected in Polvo for Barrilito's widow. Afterward, we drove Pachá to the bank to open an account. I had used the telephone number on the business card Gregorio Suarez had given me to make one call and the Ojinaga policeman had agreed to "encourage" the five Soto sons to let Pachá keep their father's casita.

Six weeks later, Ella Spivey returned home for the funeral of the eldest Spivey sister, Viola, who died from a cerebral hemorrhage, but she returned to Florida and within a year married a wealthy widower.

For the other Spivey sisters, life remained much as it had been. Leila suffered a stroke, but was said to be recovering. The Spiveys kept their word about establishing a foundation, and Texas A&M University made arrangements as planned.

Deputy Sheriff Dennis Bustamente dropped by the trading post to mention that with the departure of Rano Johnson to Mexico, the Presidio County crime wave receded, and then dried up.

Rano Johnson made his last trip across the river when his body was returned to this side for burial. The bullet-ridden body had been dumped near the bridge on the other side.

Johnson's widow married a Border Patrol agent. I saw her new husband laughing and playing baseball with Rano's sons outside their house in Presidio.

Shortly after, *The International*, in its Ojinaga section, ran a story announcing the new captain of the Municipal Police. I clipped Gregorio Esparza's photograph and pinned it to the bulletin board in the trading post.

Following Boots's death, my customers did not complain about Phobe, but they did react. Pablo Pacheco's mother forbade him to visit, even with her. Other mothers made clear that they were nervous and asked if I would lock up the bobcat before they came into the trading post. We kept her in our quarters for three months, but Phobe missed the free run of the wide aisles and suffered from her confinement. Though it hurt our hearts, on a sunny day in January, we put a squirming Phobe into her carrier, loaded it into the pickup, and drove her to La Brisa, my father's ranch. There in the warm and wind-sheltered dip between two hills, in front of the weathered clapboard house, we watched Woo Hoo, the short-legged, brown-and-white, mostly-terrier mutt, and Willie, the fat gray neutered tomcat, meet Phobe.

The bobcat stepped from the carrier and sniffed the scent-laden air. Woo Hoo, held by my kneeling father, Justice Ricciotti, wagged his tail like a whip and pulled free. He approached Phobe from the position of the inferior, head lowered, tail between his legs. Stopping right in front of her, he flattened himself on the ground, head between his paws. Phobe moved forward until they touched noses. Woo Hoo groveled in delight, making whining noises to let her know he was harmless.

Willie and Phobe met stiff-legged, fur on end, and hissing. After a few minutes' standoff, Willie slowly turned and, all the while looking back over his shoulder at Phobe, crept away to his chair on the front porch.

"Let's take them inside," my father said, smiling down at the dog and bobcat, his taut-skinned face relaxed, his nervous hands still for the present. "Willie will come around. He's just jealous of Woo Hoo having a new friend."

By the time we were ready to go home, Phobe and Woo Hoo had exhausted each other playing games of chase, hide-and-seek, and tag all over the house. Willie had come around enough to swat his paw at both whenever they ran by the safety zone of my father's lap. And my dear father, so loath to suffer human company, seemed pleased at having another animal companion. We left him sitting on the couch, Willie still in his lap, Woo Hoo leaning against him on one side, Phobe on the other, all four with sleepy eyes and contented faces.

Try as I might, I couldn't help shedding tears as we drove away. Clay leaned across and squeezed my shoulder. "You know this is best for Phobe. In a few months, folks will settle down, and we'll bring her back home with us."

"I'm not crying because we're leaving her with Dad. I'm crying because she settled in so fast and looked so happy. She may not want to come home."

Clay smiled broadly. "As a kid, did you ever go to summer camp?"

"From Polvo? We didn't even know there were such things."

"Well, every summer for six weeks, I went off to camp. As much as I loved it, I was always ready to go home. Trust me, it's like Phobe's at camp. She'll thrive, but she'll be ready to come home. I promise."